DESTINATION BOOT HILL

Wayne Coulter rode with a gang until an ambush left him wounded, and he might have died if it hadn't been for Henry Mallen and his granddaughter Julie. However, Mallen and Julie are also in trouble, and when Mallen is shot dead, Coulter takes on Julie's enemies. But when a former gang member betrays the outlaws for reward money — it means death. Gun smoke and hot lead will rage in a lethal storm to the very end . . .

PETER MALLETT

DESTINATION BOOT HILL

Complete and Unabridged

LINFORD
Leicester

First published in Great Britain in 2007 by
Robert Hale Limited
London

First Linford Edition
published 2008
by arrangement with
Robert Hale Limited
London

The moral right of the author has been asserted

British Library CIP Data

Mallett, Peter
 Destination Boot Hill.—Large print ed.—
 Linford western library
 1. Western stories
 2. Large type books
 I. Title
 823.9'2 [F]

 ISBN 978–1–84782–168–3

Published by
F. A. Thorpe (Publishing)
Anstey, Leicestershire

Set by Words & Graphics Ltd.
Anstey, Leicestershire
Printed and bound in Great Britain by
T. J. International Ltd., Padstow, Cornwall

This book is printed on acid-free paper

1

Wayne Coulter was uneasy; nerves taut and right hand gripping the butt of his holstered .45. Rain was slashing down, filling the night with disconcerting noise that could conceal other more ominous sounds — like the approach of members of the local law department. He glanced around in the uncertain gloom, his keen blue eyes picking out the motionless figure of Blackjack Dawson, the outlaw gang boss and notorious bank robber, who was standing almost within an arm's length, his massive shoulders hunched against the rain, his slicker gleaming wetly in the dim light of the single lantern suspended from an overhead beam of the railroad depot on the edge of Peyton Junction, a cow town in Kansas.

They were standing in the shadow of the telegraph office, with other members of the gang deployed along the depot in positions from which they could attack the train when it pulled in. Coulter experienced an overwhelming urge to throw in his hand and pull stakes. He had been turning against the thought of continuing his crooked way of life ever since Blackjack had taken on extra men to help with their growing nefarious activities, for one of the newcomers, Luke Doyle, had the shifty-eyed look of a disloyal man about him, although Blackjack had vouched for Doyle's sincerity.

'Blackjack,' Coulter said in a harsh whisper.

'Not now, Wayne.' Dawson lifted a commanding hand. 'Did you hear the whistle out on the flats? The train is coming.'

'All the more reason to call this off before it's too late, Boss. I got a bad feeling about this. Let's pull out, but fast.'

'Are you losing your nerve?' Dawson half turned to gaze at Coulter. 'You ain't turning yeller on me, are you, Wayne?'

'You know I ain't.' Coulter wiped rain from his face. 'It's that damn Doyle. He's a bad man.'

'Huh, show me a good man among us!' Dawson laughed deep in his throat.

'You know what I mean.' Anger edged Coulter's tone. 'I've stood by you for ten years, Blackjack, and you just got to listen to me. This is Doyle's idea, not yours, and he could have set us up for the law. There's a big price on your head these days, and I reckon Doyle is planning to collect it.'

'Nobody lives forever, Wayne. Hell, I've known all my life that I'm on the trail to Boot Hill; will probably be shot in the back, and a number of men have tried to put me there but I'm still alive and kicking at fifty-two. Just stow that kind of talk and let's hit this train like Doyle arranged. He reckons there'll be twenty thousand dollars aboard, and that ain't hay.'

Coulter lapsed into silence, his instincts warning vibrantly against the raid. He loved the incorrigible gang boss like a father, ever since Blackjack saved his life in a range war in which his parents had succumbed. They had grown close over the years, even when Blackjack had forsaken his life as a professional gambler to embark on the even more hazardous calling of robbing banks. Blackjack had proved to possess an instinctive sense of self-preservation that was uncanny in its accuracy, until he had taken on Luke Doyle, who quickly inveigled himself into the gang as a more than able henchman despite Coulter's doubts.

'There's that whistle again,' Blackjack whispered hoarsely, his harsh voice cutting through Coulter's thoughts. 'The train will be here in a few minutes. Get ready, Wayne.'

'I don't wanta go through with this, Blackjack.' Coulter spoke through his clenched teeth. 'I've got a hunch that's choking me. Something is wrong with this whole deal Doyle has cooked up. Bill Sitter told me he saw Doyle talking to a stranger in Newton last week who looked mighty like a lawman.'

'Now you tell me!' Blackjack half turned and seized Coulter's left wrist in a crushing grip. 'Why in hell have you been brooding about this until now, when it's too late to call it off? You should have spoken out before. I've seen the way you've been acting around Doyle and I figured it was jealousy because Doyle wormed his way into the gang with his slick ideas.'

'It ain't like that! I'd go through Hell for you, Blackjack, and you know it. But you're blind as far as Doyle is concerned, and I've been watching him closely. He's a wrong 'un, and we better pull out of this before I'm proved right.'

'I've worked with Doyle before this.' Blackjack fell silent when he spotted the glare of the headlight on the approaching locomotive cutting through the driving rain.

The long train rumbled into the dimly lit station, rattling to a halt with the engine level with the end of the platform. Steam hissed in a rising cloud that drifted quickly across the rail depot.

'Let's get to it.' Blackjack drew his pistol from under his streaming slicker. He retained his powerful grip on Coulter's left wrist and dragged the younger man forward from their cover despite Coulter's efforts to hang back. 'Come on. Wayne, Bill and Sam are climbing aboard the engine and Chuck and Tom will be covering the caboose. Let's hit that express car.'

A fusillade of shots hammered through the silence with shocking suddenness. Coulter's head jerked to the right towards the engine, and he saw Bill and Sam pitching backwards off the footplate as a lethal storm of hot lead blasted them. At that instant the door of the express car slid open and armed men crowded forward into the doorway. Blackjack was running towards the express car, dragging Coulter along with him, and the gang boss flinched away like a nervous pronghorn as guns flashed and boomed and bullets crackled through the night.

'It's a trap!' Blackjack yelled, his voice buffeted by the uproar. He shied away and hurled himself into the cover of the telegraph office, pulling Coulter with him.

The shooting raged in unabated fury. Coulter felt the strike of a slug in the back of his left shoulder as he fled, and stumbled as a lightning flash of pain seared through him. He heard Blackjack cry out in agony as they both fell heavily and lay together in shock.

'What in hell is going on?' rasped Blackjack, his voice hoarse with pain. 'The train is loaded with lawmen. They were waiting for us, Wayne, but how in hell did they know we were coming? We never stopped anywhere on the ride in. We travelled at night and avoided all the towns.'

'Ask Doyle,' Coulter replied, stifling a groan as he pushed himself to his knees. The shooting had ceased as suddenly as it began. 'I reckon he's the only one still standing. I saw Bill and Sam dropping off the engine. Lawmen

7

were even waiting on the footplate. We better get out of here, Blackjack.'

'I can't move, Wayne. I took a slug in the back and my legs ain't got any feeling in them.'

'I'm hit in the back of the left shoulder,' Coulter responded. He attempted to move, and pain flashed through into his chest from the shoulder blade. He stifled a groan and forced himself to his feet.

He peered through the slashing rain, saw dark figures jumping off the train and begin moving outwards in a determined search for survivors of the gang. He bent over Blackjack's huddled figure, his left arm useless as he ignored the pain of his wound, and seized hold of the big gang boss to haul him to his feet. He got his right shoulder into Blackjack's left armpit, took most of the man's weight, and hurriedly left the scene, staggering through rainladen shadows to where they had left their horses.

'It's no use; I can't make it,' Blackjack

groaned. 'Go on and save yourself, Wayne. If Doyle has fooled me then I deserve to get caught. I'm shot through and like to die. Get the hell outa here, son, but make sure you find out what happened to Doyle. You know what to do if he did turn us over to the law.'

Coulter ignored the order and half-carried Dawson through the shadows. A gun crashed somewhere along the train, and answering shots rang out as the survivors of the gang tried to make their escape. Coulter stumbled and pitched to the ground, stifling a groan at the impact. Dawson's heavy body pinned him down and he had to use all of his strength to get from under. He pressed a hand against Dawson's chest and horror stabbed through him when he failed to find a heartbeat. Blackjack Dawson was dead.

Voices were calling through the gloom, alerting Coulter to his dangerous position, and he dragged himself upright and staggered away from the spot, lurching into the night like a wounded animal. At his back an excited voice yelled that Dawson was dead.

Coulter reached two horses and hauled himself into his saddle. He hung over the neck of the bay and set the animal into motion, clinging desperately as his senses gyrated and unconsciousness threatened to betray him. Agony flared through his left shoulder at each step the horse took, but he stayed with it and moved away into the safety of black distance, aware that the slashing rain would wipe out his tracks. All he had to do was keep moving, and morning should find him safely in the clear.

The bay continued through the night, unguided some of the time, when Coulter's senses failed him and he clung to the saddle in semi-conscious state, and only the throbbing pain of his wound kept a small corner of his senses alert. He almost fell to the ground on a number of occasions, and lost all track of time, until, finally, the bay stopped suddenly and he pitched to the ground, his senses departing abruptly, leaving him unaware of his surroundings and finally free of pain . . .

A weak sun was shining through wispy clouds when Coulter opened his eyes again and became aware of his predicament. A deep silence hung over the range, and for long moments he wondered if he had died in the night, but when he attempted to move he experienced nagging pain, and felt as if he had been staked to the ground through the shoulder. His thoughts began turning and he recalled that Blackjack Dawson had died back there at the railroad depot. He closed his eyes and wished he were dead. Nothing seemed to matter, except the knowledge that Luke Doyle had betrayed them; led them into a trap, and he needed to get up and look for Doyle to finish him for his act of treachery.

He tried to move, first his legs and then the rest of his body, and quickly realized that his left shoulder was the centre of his great discomfort. He rolled on to his right side, gritting his teeth as pain was generated by the movement, and then pushed himself to his knees, his left arm falling uselessly to his side. He had to make several attempts to rise before he finally stood erect, and swayed as dizziness assailed him. He staggered, almost fell, and then looked around with narrowed gaze to take stock of his situation.

There was no sign of his horse. The range stretched away in great undulations, drying out now as the sun burned through the clouds. He saw a narrow trail off to his right and staggered towards it, holding his left elbow in his cupped right hand with his left hand resting across his chest to ease his pain. He fell when he reached the trail, and lost his senses, to be brought back to hazy reality by a hand grasping him.

Coulter looked up into a wizened face that was the colour of mahogany, and saw faded blue eyes filled with concern. The man was old, slightly built, and dressed in rough work clothes. A battered, weather-stained Stetson was pulled low over grey hair.

'Looks like you've been in a war, mister,' the oldster remarked. 'Did your hoss run off? Just lie still while I take a look at you. Say, you got a bad wound there. You must have lost a lot of blood. I reckon we better take you into town and get Doc Tracey to run the rule over you. What happened? Was you drygulched by some of Jethro Henderson's bully boys?'

'Never heard of Henderson,' Coulter mumbled. 'I don't need to see the doctor; don't wanta go to town, either.'

'Like that, huh?' The oldster chuckled. 'Say, was you caught in that shooting at the railroad depot last night? They do say Blackjack Dawson finally got his comeuppance. Well, he had a good run, by all accounts. There's a big posse out looking for the outlaws who got away, but Sheriff Coombe couldn't find any tracks to follow — rain washed them out. And if the sheriff is after you then I ain't giving you up, young feller. I'm Henry Mallen, and that damn sheriff ain't my idea of a lawman, not nohow. Anything he is for then I'm against. Come on; let's get you to my place. My granddaughter, Julie, has had some practice nursing, and she'll patch you up.'

Coulter could not reply. His senses were spinning as the old man helped him to the wagon. He sprawled forward on to the wagon bed and lay inert, his senses moving in and out of unconsciousness. The jolting of the wagon hurt him until reality faded and he passed out.

When he came to again the jolting of the wagon had ceased. He had a little trouble ungluing his eyes, and hurt his shoulder when he craned his neck to look around to discover that he was on a bed in a large room. Bright sunlight was streaming in through a small window. He was feeling strangely comfortable after the agony of his wound and wondered where he was and how he had arrived, until he recalled Henry Mallen and the mention of a granddaughter, Julie.

He drowsed into an uneasy sleep, and when he awoke again he saw a young woman at his side, gazing worriedly at him. He blinked, thinking that he was dreaming, and she leaned forward to place a cool hand on his fevered brow. He closed his eyes and heaved a great sigh.

'I'm Julie Wade,' she said, her voice sounding as if it came from a great distance. 'My grandfather found you out on the trail. You've been shot back in the left shoulder. The bullet went right through. I've cleaned the wound, but you should be attended by the doctor. You've been in a fever for the last two days.'

'No doctor,' he mumbled. 'Say, have I been here two days?'

'Three.' She smiled, and he looked more intently at her, realizing that she was young, no more than eighteen years old. She was dark-haired, and had brown eyes that seemed filled with sadness. He wondered what was worrying her, aware that most folks had some kind of trouble these days. 'You've been very lucky,' she continued. 'Another inch to the right and you would have died on the spot.' She paused and busied herself for a moment, pulling his pillow straight and smoothing down the blanket that covered him. 'Were you in that gunfight the other night at the rail depot in Peyton Junction?'

'I got caught up in some shooting,' he admitted cautiously.

'Do you mean you were passing by and got involved?' she persisted. 'What I'm trying to get at is are you a gunman working for Jethro Henderson? He's making life difficult for us, him and his hardcases.'

'I never heard of Henderson,' Coulter said flatly.

'So you are an outlaw.' She waited for a reply but he remained silent.

'Don't worry about it, if you are,' she went on. 'Grandpa wouldn't ever hand you over to the law. He hates Sheriff

Coombe, and wouldn't miss a chance to put one over on that fat hog. We'll get you back on your feet and you can go on your way. You were lying on the trail, Grandpa said. What happened to your horse?'

'I guess it kept going when I finally fell out of the saddle.'

'I found a horse two days ago, eating hay in our corral. What colour is your animal?'

'It's a bay.'

'I guessed it was your horse. There was blood on the saddle. I've hidden it in a draw back of the house. Will you take some soup? You must be ravenous now.'

Coulter closed his eyes as she left the room, his senses drifting, but Julie returned and began spooning soup into his mouth. Afterwards, Coulter slept restlessly, his feverish movements sending agonies of pain through his wound. Night came and passed and morning followed. Daylight brought him back to stark reality and he looked at Julie, his feverish gaze unsteady, his blue eyes dark-circled.

Julie checked his wound, and he watched her anxiously, saw her shake her head.

'Is it healing?' he demanded.

'It's getting better, but I don't like the look of it. I think we should send for Doc Tracey. If poison sets in, nothing will save you.' A trace of bitterness sounded in her voice. 'I know what I'm talking about,' she hurried on when he began to protest. 'My father was shot last year by one of Jethro Henderson's hardcases. We didn't get the doctor over to check him, and he died a week later.'

'I'll take my chances without the doc,' Coulter insisted.

'You can trust Doc Tracey. He wouldn't tell the law of your presence here. He has no love for the sheriff either.'

'No doctor,' Coulter repeated. 'Has the law been around?'

'No, but Coombe will pay us a visit; no doubt about that. He has business

18

interests with Henderson, who has gobbled up the town and has started turning his attention to the range, and Coombe will follow his own brand of law-dealing to see that Henderson comes out on top. Murder has been committed around here, and if the victims have been against Henderson then the killers are never pursued.'

'Is that a fact?' Coulter closed his eyes and lapsed into sleep. Fever gripped him and he tossed and turned restlessly through three more days, tended ceaselessly by Julie, who sponged his forehead repeatedly and checked his wound incessantly for the first signs of dreaded poison.

On the fourth day, Coulter opened his eyes under the pressure of pain spearing though his left shoulder, and was alarmed by the sight of an intent bearded face peering down at him. He attempted to rise but a heavy hand pressed him back, and he saw Julie's haggard face in the background, looking on worriedly.

'Just stay still,' the man ordered. 'I'm

Doc Tracey. Think yourself lucky Julie finally had the sense to call me in. I'm about through tending you. It looks like you've come through the worst of it. A week ago there was an attempted robbery at the railroad depot. And that's about the time you collected this wound. I ain't heard of any other shooting around here, so I'm putting two and two together. Sheriff Coombe was talking last night about the Dawson gang. Six of them were killed by Pinkerton detectives and lawmen in the gun trap they set up, but Coombe reckons a couple of the desperadoes got away, and he's got posses out around the county looking for them. He reckons none of them got away unwounded. Has Coombe showed up here yet, Julie?'

'He wouldn't set foot on this place with Grandpa standing guard,' Julie replied.

Doc Tracey chuckled. He was tall and broad-shouldered, probably in his mid-fifties, and his capable hands did not waver as he bandaged Coulter's shoulder. When he had completed the task he closed his leather medical bag and stepped back from the bed.

'I'll drop by and see you again in a couple of days,' he said. 'You're on the mend now but you better stay where you are until your pain has gone. Take it easy when you do start moving around. Julie will call me in if you take a turn for the worse.'

'Thanks, Doc,' Coulter responded. 'What do I owe you?'

'Wait until you're on your feet,' Doc Tracey concluded. 'I'll call and see you again.'

When the doctor had departed, Coulter looked around the room. He was feeling sharper now, and more alert. He saw his gunbelt and pistol hanging from a hook in the door. Julie returned, and Coulter stifled a groan as he tried to push himself into a sitting position. Julie hurried to his side.

'What are you doing?' she demanded in alarm. 'You heard what the doctor said. You've got to rest several more days.'

'I've got to get out of here before the doc gets back to town and reports me,' Coulter said harshly. 'Where are my clothes? I need to be hitting the trail, but fast. I'll have to be two jumps ahead of a posse to stand any chance of getting away. I'm obliged for the way you looked after me, but it's time I was on the move. I've already been in one place too long, and you could get into a lot of trouble if the law found out that you took me in.'

'You're not going anywhere,' she insisted. 'Doc Tracey won't report you. Just lie still and rest or you'll undo all the good I've done so far.'

'Get me my gunbelt,' he insisted. 'I can't defend myself with it hanging on the door. Have you got my saddle-bags? I need to clean the pistol, just in case we have visitors.'

Julie eyed him doubtfully for some moments, then sighed and fetched his gunbelt. Coulter drew the .45 pistol and examined it. There were spots of rust on the cylinder and the barrel. He broke the gun and unloaded it. Julie picked up his saddle-bags from a corner of the room, came to place them on the bed, and then departed, her worried face showing disapproval.

Coulter opened a bag and produced cleaning materials. He worked the gun, using one hand, and groaned each time he inadvertently moved his left shoulder and caused pain to flare in it. He felt easier when he had finished the chore, and hung the belt over a bed post with the butt of the gun close to his right side. He dragged himself up the bed slightly in order to peer out the window, and gazed longingly at a short stretch of the trail leading away from the little ranch.

He fell to thinking about the abortive train raid, and decided that the first thing he had to do when he was on his feet again was hunt down Luke Doyle. He had no doubt that Doyle had sold out Blackjack and the gang.

His thoughts were bitter as he considered his future. Blackjack Dawson had been like a father to him for ten years, and now he was on his own with no idea what to do. He had become a robber only because that was the profession of his mentor, and with Blackjack gone he would no longer live outside the law.

He slept again, and awoke when daylight had gone and black velvet night held sway over the range. Julie brought him hot food and he was able to sit up and feed himself. He was weak and needed nourishment, but the signs were that he was improving steadily. When Julie returned for his plate he was in a sombre mood.

'I guess I'm well enough to thank you for what you're doing for me,' he said. 'There's a roll of bills in my vest pocket. Take what you think I owe you for the nursing.'

'I saw your money. It's under your pillow. I washed your clothes. The shirt was badly bloodstained but I got most

24

of it out. You don't owe us a thing. Just take it easy and heal up properly, and then you can be on your way. I shall be glad to see the back of you. If the sheriff does come nosing around while you're here it could be bad for Grandpa. Henderson is looking for reasons why we should be kicked out of here, and harbouring a criminal would give him a good reason to move in against us.'

Coulter considered her words, and realized why she was looking so worried.

'I wouldn't want to bring trouble down on you,' he said. 'I'll pull out in the morning. I'll be OK if I take it easy.'

'You don't have to leave until you're completely healed. You could run into a posse if you go too soon. The sheriff will call off the hunt, and that will be time enough for you to go. Do you have a name? There was nothing in your saddle-bags to identify you. I was thinking that if you had died on us we couldn't notify your family. You must have parents somewhere.'

'No,' he said softly. 'I don't have a living soul. As to a name, just call me Jack Smith. I'll answer to that.'

Julie shook her head as she left him. Coulter settled down in the bed and drifted into slumber. The sun was shining when he next opened his eyes, and he wondered what had disturbed him. Then he heard a harsh voice talking very loudly just outside the window and, as he reached for his pistol, a shot hammered with shocking suddenness and echoed sullenly through the early morning . . .

2

Pain cut through Coulter's wound as he turned hurriedly and snatched his pistol from its holster. He cursed and slid out of bed, staggering as he cocked the gun. The echoes of the shot were fading into the distance as he eased against the wall beside the window and peered outside to see a man standing in the yard with a hand pressing against his right shoulder; blood was showing through his splayed fingers. Coulter saw a pistol lying in the dust and noted a saddle horse standing with trailing reins in the background. Then he heard Henry Mallen's voice, and saw the rancher appearing in his line of vision. Mallen was holding a Winchester in his hands.

'Why in hell are you snooping around here, Carson? I told you I'd gut-shoot any of Henderson's crew if I caught them on my range.'

'Yuh crazy old coot! I was sent here with a message.'

'And you came into my yard with a drawn pistol to deliver it,' Mallen jeered. 'You were hoping to get the drop on me, you polecat, and there's no saying what hell you'd have got up to if I'd been asleep. Go on and get outa here before I put a slug in you where you can't digest it. Tell Henderson I ain't selling out and I won't quit. Tell your outfit I'm loaded for bear, and I'll toss lead at anyone who shows up.'

Carson turned, staggered to his horse, and hauled himself into the saddle. He left his pistol lying in the dust when he rode away, slumped over his saddle horn. Coulter heard Julie's voice raised in anger as she upbraided Mallen for shooting Carson.

'It was lucky I got him first,' the old man retorted. 'We could have been murdered in our beds if I hadn't been watching for trouble.'

'Carson might die on the trail,' Julie protested. 'You should have let me take a look at him before running him out.'

'No dice! I don't want any JH rider making tracks in the dust of my yard. Henderson has made his intentions plain, and he's gonna have to fight for this place, if he wants it.'

'Grandpa, they could run all over us and not notice us in passing if Henderson so minded. You're not helping the situation with your defiant attitude. What did Carson come here for? You didn't give him a chance to explain.'

Coulter uncocked his gun and crawled back into bed. His shoulder was aching as he returned his pistol to its holster. He lay listening to Julie and her grandpa arguing over the situation, and suddenly felt impatient to hit the trail. He got out of bed again, hunted for his clothes, found them in a cupboard, and dressed slowly, grunting as each movement hurt his shoulder. He was pulling on his boots when the door opened and Julie entered the room.

'I'm sorry you were disturbed. Grandpa was watching for trouble and Hank Carson, of the Henderson outfit, showed up, so Grandpa shot him.'

'I looked out the window and saw Carson. I don't blame your grandpa for keeping watch. If you've got a problem with your neighbour then you have to expect trouble at any time.'

'How are you feeling now you're up and dressed?'

'Not good, but it'll get better,' he assured her. 'I need to be riding out of here. I'll only add to your trouble if I'm caught on the spread.'

'I don't think you're well enough to ride yet. You won't get a mile down the trail before your wound breaks open, and then you'll be back where you started. Take it easy around the place for a couple more days and then you'll have a better chance of making it away. I know what I'm talking about. I remember my father when I was nursing him. He thought he knew better than me, and died.'

30

'You saved my life, and the last thing I'd wanta do is bring trouble down on you.' Coulter shook his head. 'I don't have to ride far. I could hole up on the range for a few days, and then get away. I just don't wanta be on your spread if the sheriff shows up with a posse.'

'Walt Coombe knows better than to ride in here. Grandpa has warned him off, and the last twice Coombe has called he's waited at the gate.'

'If he's looking for outlaws then he'll ride right in and stomp through the house,' Coulter insisted. 'I got a hunch that I'd better be riding.' He reached under the pillow on the bed and produced his wad of greenbacks. 'Tell me what I owe you for your trouble and sell me some supplies, and I'll head out fast.'

'I don't want paying for what I've done.' Julie looked downcast. 'Come and have some breakfast, and then see how you feel. I could show you a place on the range where you could stay for a couple of days, if you're really set on quitting the house.'

'That might be a good idea.' Coulter moved his shoulder gingerly and clenched his teeth against the pain that stabbed through it. He followed Julie through to the big living room and saw Henry Mallen standing just inside the open doorway, peering out across the range, his rifle in his hands.

'Howdy, young feller,' Henry greeted. 'Glad to see you up and about at last. I reckon we'll be getting a visit from the sheriff any day now. I heard he was over to the west of us yesterday. He's sure keen on picking up the two outlaws who got away from that train robbery. Joe Ketchell dropped by last evening on his way from town and said Coombe told him one of the outlaws informed on the gang and set up the gun trap that killed Blackjack Dawson.'

'Yeah. Luke Doyle.' Coulter spoke through clenched teeth.

'That's the name Ketchell mentioned. Did you know it was Doyle?'

'I guessed at the last moment.'

Coulter shook his head. 'The first thing I'm gonna do when I'm fit to travel is look up Doyle.'

'He's living in Peyton Junction right now, spending the dough he got for turning in the gang,' Mallen said. 'But you better not ride in there after him just yet. He's got more deputies around him than a dog's got fleas.'

Coulter sat down at the table and ate the meal Julie placed before him. She sat opposite him, her expression proclaiming that she was not happy with his decision to ride. Henry Mallen remained just inside the doorway, peering around a doorpost with his rifle ready in his hands.

'I knew it,' the oldster said suddenly. 'I got a nose for trouble, and the air sure smelled bad when I got up this morning. Carson came in to look around, and now some more of Henderson's gunnies are coming up.'

Coulter got to his feet and moved to a window. He saw three riders approaching the yard, moving at a trot, and two of them were holding drawn weapons. Julie came to his side and Coulter turned on her.

'You'd better hunt up some cover,' he said grimly. 'It looks like they're loaded for bear.'

'Why don't you take Julie and make it out the back door?' Mallen suggested.

'I'll take a look out back,' Julie said. 'If they're coming to attack us then there'll be more of them cutting us off. She turned and ran through to the kitchen, and a moment later she exclaimed: 'There are two riders coming in at the back.'

'Will you cover the back, young feller?' Mallen asked.

Coulter drew his pistol and went through to the kitchen. Julie was peering out the window. He joined her, and saw two riders coming in close with drawn guns. Coulter motioned for Julie to get back. He checked his pistol. The riders drew nearer and, suddenly, Henry Mallen was shooting his rifle, sending a string of hammering shots across the front yard.

The riders facing Coulter dismounted when the shots sounded out front and came at a run towards the back door, raising their weapons and triggering shots at the house. Coulter broke a window pane with his gun barrel. Bullets thudded into the woodwork around the window where he was standing. He lifted his pistol and started shooting, hardly seeming to aim the weapon as it bucked and recoiled against the heel of his hand. Gun smoke drifted and his ears protested at the shock of the shooting.

The nearest man twisted and pitched to the ground. Coulter shifted his aim quickly. His muzzle covered the second man as it exploded, and a speeding bullet sent the attacker sprawling with blood showing on his chest. Coulter turned and ran through to the front room, for Henry Mallen was shooting continuously.

Gun smoke was drifting thickly around the doorway, where Mallen was

35

standing openly, working the mechanism of his rifle and spraying hot lead across the yard. Coulter moved to a window. His gaze narrowed when he saw a man down in the dust and the other two advancing at a run, determined to get to close quarters.

Coulter cut loose with his .45, emptying the pistol in a burst of shooting that sent one of the men sprawling. Mallen got the last man, dropping him only a few yards from the open doorway. Coulter turned to the old man and saw him bleeding from a chest wound. Mallen was slumping, his rifle falling from his hands, and he pitched forward on his face. A trickle of blood showed on the dusty floorboards.

Julie gave a shocked cry and came hurrying to her grandfather's side. She turned him on to his back, dropped to her knees beside him, and unbuttoned his blood-soaked shirt. Coulter, peering at the small man over the girl's shoulder, could see at a glance that he was dead. Julie regained her feet, her face set in a mask of shock and horror. She picked up the rifle Mallen had dropped and checked its mechanism before turning to look out across the yard.

'There'll be more of them coming soon,' she said in a weary tone. 'Henderson has been threatening for a long time to kick us out. We told the sheriff about it but there was no help coming from that direction.' She looked into Coulter's face, her eyes calm, filled with resignation and tinged with horor. 'You'd better get out of here while you can. Take it easy for a few days, until you get your strength back.'

'I ain't riding out if you're set on staying,' Coulter broke his pistol and reloaded the spent chambers from the loops on his cartridge belt.

'It's not your fight,' she protested, 'and you'll surely be killed in the next attack. Henderson has got twenty riders on his payroll; all tough, fighting men, and they've always been more than ready to use their guns. They've practically cleared this range of small ranchers. Grandpa wouldn't let them bully him, but the axe has fallen at last, and I shall soon be knee-deep in hardcases. Do like I say and pull out quick. You need to be well away from here by the time they come again.'

'I'll leave if you'll go with me,' Coulter replied. 'If you won't budge then I'll stay and we'll go down together. My parents were killed in a range war so I hate Henderson without even knowing him. I'll fight him on principle, and I won't quit while there's shooting to be done.'

He stepped out to the porch and looked around. The bodies out in the dust of the yard were motionless. He sighed long and hard as he looked around. This was not his fight but there was no way he could depart and leave Julie to what he knew would come. She had saved his life and he would die to save her if that was what was on the cards.

Julie came out to the porch, carrying

a rifle. Her face was pale and set, her teeth clenched, and she hardly moved her lips when she spoke.

'I've thought it over. I can't stay here if you won't leave. I'll move out now. If I'm gonna continue this fight then I need to get smart. I'll lay up somewhere, and wait until I can get the drop on Henderson. He doesn't know it, but he won't live to enjoy his landgrabbing. I'll do the job Grandpa always promised to do — put Henderson down in the dust.'

'We'd better move fast,' Coulter urged. 'Take anything with you that you wouldn't want to fall into Henderson's hands, and let's split the breeze.'

Julie went back into the house. Coulter followed, and saw her lift a stone in the hearth to reveal a cavity. She picked up a small wooden box and continued through to the kitchen, where she collected some provisions in a gunny sack. At the back door she paused and looked at Coulter.

'I'm ready,' she said quietly. 'There's

nothing else here that I could carry, so let's go.'

Coulter collected his rifle and saddle-bags from the bedroom while Julie collected cooking implements. He followed her out to the barn at the rear of the house, and had to stand watching helplessly while she saddled a horse. His wounded shoulder was aching intolerably but he set his teeth and ignored the pain. When they set out across the back yard Coulter turned aside, picked up a broom, and blotted out the tracks they were leaving in the thick dust. They continued across the range, Coulter walking behind Julie's horse, and did not pause until they were behind the cover of a ridge some 300 yards from the deserted ranch house.

Julie paused and looked back at the little ranch, her lips compressed, her eyes filled with shock. Coulter watched her with narrowed gaze. He was filled with sympathy for her plight, but said nothing, aware that anything he could say would not help her at that moment.

'You're looking a bit peaky,' she observed, gazing at him. 'It's your first time out of bed since you were wounded, and you should be resting instead of running. Your horse is in a draw in the high ground about a mile away. I've been taking care of him. I rode him a few times to keep him fit. We'd better rest up there today and see what you feel like in the morning. If you can ride then we'll make for our line shack on Alder Creek and you'll be able to take it easy there until you get your strength back. I don't think Henderson's hardcases will bother to check out the shack.'

Coulter nodded. He took a last look around at the little ranch lying silent and still in the middle distance. His eyes were bleak as he turned and followed Julie along a game trail that led into rising ground. By the time they reached the draw where his bay was hidden he was tottering and almost out of his head. He dropped to the ground

41

and lay unmoving for long minutes, wondering if he would ever regain his strength, but as time passed he recovered sufficiently to sit up.

Julie was seated opposite, watching him, and she smiled wanly as their gazes met.

'Feeling better now?' she asked.

He nodded. 'I couldn't ride at all today,' he mused, 'but I should be all right tomorrow. I'll rest now, and take another walk later. I'll soon get over this.' He paused, watching her. 'What about you? Do you have any folks you can go to?'

'There's no one, and if there was I wouldn't leave this range.' She spoke strongly. 'All I'm interested in at the moment is shooting Henderson.'

'That's not a woman's work.' Coulter shook his head. 'I owe you my life, Julie, and I always pay my debts. I'll kill Henderson for you, and you can watch if it will make you feel any better. It won't bother me none to do the chore, but we'll have to pick the time and place carefully, for we won't get a second chance if we foul up the first time. I think we should wait a couple of weeks before making our try. It will give the situation time to settle. When the smoke has cleared we'll move in and do the job, and then get the hell out. How does that sound to you?'

'I don't want you to get involved.' She shook her head. 'You're in enough trouble on your own account. That man Doyle is still in Peyton Junction, and he could recognize you.'

'So I've got two chores to handle,' Coulter said. 'Henderson and Doyle. That's OK by me. Now I'd better try and get some sleep. My shoulder is aching real bad.'

He stretched out on the hard ground and closed his eyes resolutely, but sleep wouldn't come and he tried to force his mind from its incessant pondering. He did fall asleep eventually, to awaken in the middle of the night. Darkness and silence surrounded him and he lifted his head to look around. Julie was a shapeless figure to his right, huddled in a blanket, and the sight of her reassured him. He lowered his head and slept again.

The sun was just clear of the horizon when he awoke once more. The bay had whinnied and disturbed him. Well versed in the ways of the animal, he drew his gun and cocked it, aware that someone was approaching. He looked around, saw Julie sitting up in her blanket with her rifle in her hand, her face gaunt, filled with fear, and warned her softly.

'Someone's moving around out there. Stay still while I take a look around.'

He eased himself to his knees; his ears strained for sound, and caught the click and thump of hoofs somewhere between them and the distant ranch. He inched his way up the side of the draw, favouring his left shoulder, and when he was able to observe the range between them and the ranch he saw two riders approaching. They were studying the ground, obviously following sign.

He relaxed and watched them coming in closer under the muzzle of his deadly gun.

Julie joined him, holding her rifle, and Coulter stuck his pistol in his belt and used his right hand to grasp the barrel of the girl's long gun.

'Don't shoot,' he warned. 'They may pass us by without trouble.'

'They're tracking us,' Julie said. 'I'll shoot them before they get too close.'

'Do you know who they are?'

'Sure. Rap Kenyon and Pete Drury — Henderson riders. It looks like they've come from my spread, so they'll have seen the dead men down there. These two have visited us several times, bullying Grandpa and tormenting me.'

'Did they put hands on you?' Coulter demanded.

'No, but they did everything short of that. They're a couple of no-goods.'

'Let's watch them for a bit. They look like they might be angling to the right. It'll be good if they go on by.'

The two riders came on steadily.

Coulter could see that both men were heavily armed, and were moving with a stiffness of manner that indicated their alertness. One was carrying a rifle across his saddle horn, and their keen eyes were studying the ground before them with an intensity that warned Coulter that they were following tracks.

'They won't ride by,' Julie said at length, jacking a cartridge into the breech of her Winchester.

'I think you're right.' Coulter took his hand off the rifle. 'I'll get the drop on them when they come closer. We'll hear what they've got to say.'

'What good will that do? Henderson's bunch declared war on me yesterday when they shot Grandpa. This is not your fight, so let me get on with it.'

'OK.' Coulter nodded. 'Shoot them.'

Julie looked at him for a long moment, and could tell by his expression that he did not think she would shoot. She sighed heavily and lifted the long gun to her shoulder. Coulter narrowed his eyes and clenched his teeth. Julie sighted the rifle. The sun glinted on the barrel. Coulter resisted the impulse to stop her at the last moment.

The crack of the shot blasted the perfect silence of the morning. Coulter saw the rider on the left jerk at the smashing impact of the speeding .44.40 slug, then pitch forward over the neck of his horse and fall heavily to the ground. The other man swung his mount quickly, and was galloping away before Julie could reload. She fired quickly, and missed.

Coulter drew his pistol and fired instantly, and a moment later the fleeing rider was down on the ground. The echoes of the shooting faded slowly as Coulter sat back on his heels and looked around, aware that the two men might be scouting for a larger party, and if that was the case then big trouble would shortly loom on the horizon.

3

They sat motionless long after the last
echoes of the shooting had died away,
watching and listening for trouble, but
nothing moved around them as the sun
pushed clear of the horizon. Coulter
finally got to his feet, pistol in his right
hand and his left hand held up across
his chest to ease his wounded shoulder.
Stabs of pain were pulsing through him
with every heart beat.

'I'll go and check those two.' He
spoke through gritted teeth. 'Stay here
and cover me. I have a nasty feeling that
more trouble will strike the minute I
put my nose outside this draw.'

'I'll cover you.' Julie's face was pale.
She was under stress, but he was
surprised by her determination and
assumed that she was acting under
great shock.

He left the draw, gun hanging loosely

down at his side in his right hand, and went to the bodies of the two men. Ascertaining that they were dead, he looked around before starting back to the draw. Nothing moved out there on the range. Silence pressed in around him. His thoughts were stagnant, and he forced himself to consider the situation. It came to him that he had very little time to get clear, and realized that he was wasting that valuable commodity. He went back to the draw.

'We've got to get out of here, but fast,' he announced. 'This place will be crawling with Henderson's men before long. You know how the land lies, so let's get moving, and pick the hardest ground you can find.'

Julie did not protest. She saddled their horses and they mounted and rode out, travelling at little more than a walk. Coulter experienced some pain in his shoulder, but it eased after some minutes and he faced his front stoically, determined to find a better hiding place. They travelled through the long hours of the morning, and he was ready to rest when they rode into a thicket and Julie called a halt. They had spoken little during the ride, for Julie had lapsed into a sombre mood, and Coulter was accustomed to riding in silence for long stretches at a time.

Coulter could do no more than lie on a blanket while Julie prepared food. He was exhausted; his left shoulder throbbed painfully, and he was glad to be out of the saddle. When a meal was ready he sat up and ate hungrily, and afterwards dropped back on the blanket and closed his eyes.

'Do you think you can go on until sundown?' Julie enquired.

Coulter opened his eyes and looked at her. She was quite composed, but there were dark circles under her eyes and her face was drawn and pale.

'We need to go on,' he responded, 'but I don't think my shoulder would appreciate it. Maybe I should rest up now and be better for travelling tomorrow.'

'That's how I see it.' She sighed heavily. 'We're only a couple of miles from town, and I'm thinking I should ride into Peyton Junction and report to Sheriff Coombe, although I know he won't do anything to help me. But my side of this trouble should be made known. I want to talk to Doc Tracey and other honest men in town so they'll know what really happened out at my place.'

'You'll come back here for me later?' Coulter enquired.

'Yes, although I don't want you to get caught up in my troubles. You've got enough on your plate as it is. You should just fade away from here when you're able to ride out, and forget about this business.'

'We'll talk about that later,' Coulter promised. He took a wad of notes from his pocket, peeled off several, and handed them to Julie. She took them reluctantly, her expression showing exactly what her feelings were about handling stolen money. 'Buy cartridges for my .45 and some .44.40 slugs for our rifles when you're in town,' he instructed, 'and get anything else you think we may need out here.'

'I'll attend to that.' Julie nodded as she stuffed the notes into a breast pocket. 'I'll load up on supplies. I reckon to ride to our line shack in the north. You'll be able to rest up there.'

'If you come across Henderson or any of his outfit in town then just keep out of their way,' he advised. 'Your best chance at them will come later, when they're not expecting trouble.'

She nodded, her expression bleak. 'I'll be back before sundown. See you later.'

Coulter watched her ride away, and was filled with misgiving as she disappeared beyond a ridge for she was in shock and would not be able to act rationally in any situation. But he was helpless, tied down by his wound, and sighed as he considered what should be done.

He slept despite his concern, awakening later to the sound of horses close by.

He saw three riders jogging along in the direction of Peyton Junction and noted that the brand on the animals was JH — Jethro Henderson's outfit. The leading rider seemed a cut above the other two; wearing good range clothes — a tall, big man with wide shoulders and a grim face that carried a bad expression. He guessed the big man was Henderson, and watched the trio closely until they disappeared over a crest. They were not looking for anyone, and did not check their surroundings as they rode at a canter.

Unable to rest, Coulter cleaned his weapons to pass the time, and waited impatiently for Julie's return, his thoughts intense as he tried to analyse his feelings about the situation, but he was instinctively aware that it was already too late to escape the consequences of what had occurred at the Mallen ranch. He was trapped in a bad situation and, despite his knowledge, all he could reason out was that he owed Julie his life for taking him in and nursing him, and he would see her through her present troubles before considering moving on, even if staying meant he would lose his life.

Darkness fell, and he became alarmed when the girl did not show up. He mounted and rode to the top of the ridge where he had last seen her, and was surprised to spot the lights of Peyton Junction in the distance. He was rested enough to be able to ride to town, and sent the horse forward at a walk, afraid of doing too much and starting up the terrible ache that attended previous attempts to exercise. He found that by holding his left arm across his chest he could tolerate the discomfort.

When he reached the fringe of the town he slid out of the saddle and hobbled the bay in a brush-choked draw just clear of town limits. Aware that it might be inviting trouble to pack a gun openly, he thrust his pistol into the waistband of his pants and put the gunbelt and empty holster in his bedroll. Satisfied that his open coat concealed the big pistol, he walked slowly along the sidewalk of the main street.

A dense blackness covered Peyton Junction, with lighted windows here and there creating small oases of yellow brilliance that made the surrounding darkness seem even denser. Coulter felt strangely vulnerable as he tugged his hat brim lower down across his alert blue eyes and walked at a leisurely gait into the collection of buildings, aware, almost instantly, of the near-impossibility of locating Julie. The girl could be any-where — visiting friends, buying provisions and ammunition, or being delayed by the local law after reporting to Sheriff Coombe the grim incidents that had occurred out at the Mallen ranch.

Staying in the shadows, Coulter passed the livery barn and reached the batwings of a brightly lit saloon. The sound of a tinkling piano came from inside as he paused and peered through a dusty window, the sound making him keenly aware that some men were able to lead a normal life. There were at least a dozen men inside, some of them dressed in range clothes, and Coulter glanced at the several horses tied to the hitch rail at the edge of the sidewalk. His lean figure tensed when he saw JH burned on the flank of the nearest animal, but the well-dressed man he assumed to be Henderson was not inside the saloon . . .

He was about to turn away when his sharp gaze began to register details of some of the men bellied up to the bar, and he stiffened when he saw a figure that looked familiar. He recognized Luke Doyle, and a tremor shook him as anger flared in his mind. He pulled his pistol from his waistband and cocked the weapon while the heat of vengeance burned in him. Then he noted that Doyle, big, brash and unscrupulous, with a huge grin on his pock-marked face, was talking animatedly to a gun-hung individual who was wearing a law star on his shirt front. A cold splash of common sense seeped into Coulter's brain and he put away his gun.

His prime task was to locate Julie and get out of town without trouble, he told himself, breathing deeply to control his wild impulse. His personal vendetta would have to wait until he was capable of pursuing it successfully. He needed to confront Doyle when the renegade was alone, and at the moment Julie's problems were more urgent than his own. He sighed long and heavily as he went on along the sidewalk.

He reached the open door of the general store. The store-keeper was closing the front door when Coulter paused and the man eyed him closely.

'You want something?' he demanded. 'I've been open since day-break. It's time now to call it a day.'

Coulter shook his head and turned away. The door was slammed at his back and he heard bolts being thrust home. He moved to the edge of the sidewalk and paused to look around, a stranger in a dark town, with no one he could approach freely with his questions. His loneliness was tangible, oppressive, as he longed for a sight of the girl who had saved his life. He set his teeth into his bottom lip as he considered.

Where was Julie? She had obviously been delayed somewhere or she would have returned to him before nightfall. He spotted the law office just along the street, its big front window brightly lit, the door standing open, the big sign over the door illuminated by a lantern hanging on a hook nearby. He moved closer, his breathing quickening as he approached.

There was an alley beside the law office and Coulter slipped into its welcome darkness. He eased forward around the corner until he could peer into the office through the dusty front window. Two men were inside. One was sitting behind a large, paper-littered desk; an immense man past middle-age whose overweight body was bloated with obesity. His face was like a full moon, all shape lost in sagging folds of flesh. His eyes were small, almost hidden in the network of wrinkles surrounding them, and he had two chins. His huge stomach bulged ominously above a wide leather belt. A sheriff's star was pinned to his massive chest.

Sheriff Coombe. The name came unbidden into Coulter's mind. He looked around the office for some sign that Julie might have been in, but there was nothing. He looked at the second man, a small, thin individual wearing a deputy star who was talking earnestly while the sheriff only half-listened.

Turning away, Coulter walked on along the side-walk until he reached the window of a restaurant. He rubbed a hole in the dust coating the pane and peered through the window. The place was filled to over-flowing, with hardly a vacant place at the dozen or so small tables. Two waitresses were moving around ceaselessly, attending to the needs of the diners, and Coulter forced

59

himself to move away despite the hunger gnawing in his stomach, his way of life having accustomed him to going hungry.

Frustration was beginning to get at Coulter as he looked around. All he wanted was to locate Julie and then pull out. He walked on, and paused eventually outside a house that had a brass nameplate beside the door bearing the legend MICHAEL TRACEY M.D.

He remembered the doctor. Tracey hadn't reported his presence to the sheriff after treating him, perhaps out of friendship for Julie and her grandfather. Coulter was desperate enough to take a chance. He knocked at the door, which was opened almost immediately by a tall, thin woman who peered intently at him.

'I'd like to see the doctor,' Coulter said.

'Come in,' she invited instantly. 'Doc has just finished his supper.'

Coulter entered the house and

removed his hat. The woman closed the door and then led the way along a carpeted hall to a door, which stood ajar.

'Someone to see you, Mike,' she announced, pushing the door open wide. She did not enter but stepped aside, and walked away as Coulter entered the room.

Doc Tracey was sitting at ease on a sofa, smoking an after-supper pipe. He peered through a cloud of smoke at Coulter and got to his feet when recognition dawned.

'I was just thinking about you,' Tracey declared. 'I wondered if you would show up. What happened out at the Mallen place yesterday? I'd only got half the story from Julie when Sheriff Coombe arrested her.'

'She's in jail?' Coulter's expression hardened. 'What in hell happened?'

'She rode in just before Henderson arrived with a couple of his gunnies. I was talking to her in front of the general store when Henderson showed. Before

I knew what was happening Julie dragged a rifle from her saddle boot and put a slug in Henderson, quick as a rattlesnake.'

'Did she kill him?'

'No. He took a flesh wound. His kind has the luck of the devil when it comes to justice. Henderson has caused a lot of trouble and misery around here. I patched him up after Coombe stuck Julie in jail. When I tried to see her, Coombe wouldn't let me near her. I talked to Vince Taylor, the local lawyer, who went to the jail to see Julie, but Coombe barred him from visiting her until tomorrow. So what happened out at the spread yesterday? Julie said Henry was shot dead.'

Coulter nodded, and narrated the events in question, his voice low-pitched and unemotional. Tracey shook his head and heaved a long sigh.

'So that's the rights of it, huh? Henderson said his men were shot at by two weapons when they rode into the Mallen spread — Henry and Julie, he supposed. He didn't know about your presence, huh, and you gave Henry a hand? You must be something special with a gun.'

'I get by.' Coulter firmed his lips as he considered. 'I'll drop by the jail and bust Julie out.'

'Just like that?' Tracey's expression showed that he disagreed with the idea. 'You could get yourself shot again, son. Looking at Sheriff Coombe, you wouldn't think he's a man of action, but Boot Hill is populated by men who underestimated him.'

'I'll do it right.' Coulter smiled. 'I'll fetch my horse into town and get Julie's from the livery barn; then I'll spring her loose and we'll split the breeze.'

'Be careful around town. Luke Doyle is living high on the hog right now, with five thousand dollars reward money in his pocket for putting the finger on Blackjack Dawson. He's got Kit Callahan, a county deputy, watching his back for him until the last two members of Blackjack Dawson's gang have been

63

captured. Doyle won't feel safe until you are dead or in jail. He's living the good life right now, and paying Coombe for protection.'

'They're looking for two members of the gang?' Coulter was surprised. 'Do you know the name of the other?'

'Sure. Al Billing. He was shot in the gun trap at the train, but got away.'

'Good old Al! I hope he kept running.'

'The sheriff is certain you and Billing are still in this neck of the woods. He's got a six-man posse out looking for sign. They're poking into every place between here and the border. You'll have your work cut out to avoid them.'

'And Doyle can put the finger on me,' Coulter mused. 'Mebbe I'd better put him down before I bust Julie out of jail.'

'The odds are too great for you to handle,' Tracey insisted. 'Henderson is in a room at the hotel, with a couple of gunnies guarding him. If you bust Julie out of jail she won't leave town until she's had another crack at Henderson. I know that gal, and she won't rest until Henderson is dead.'

'I'll play the cards as they fall,' Coulter decided. 'Thanks for the information, Doc.'

'I'll help you get Julie out of jail,' Tracey offered.

'You better stay out of it.' Coulter shook his head. 'I'll see Julie in the clear. She saved my life and I owe her a big favour. Leave it to me, Doc.'

Tracey shook his head. 'Times are bad when a man like Henderson can ride roughshod over his neighbours and get away with it. The sheriff should put a stop to the crookedness, but he's in with Henderson.'

'Mebbe not.' Coulter turned to depart. Tracey put out a restraining hand.

'Before you go, son, I'd better take a look at that wound you're packing. You should have rested up a few more days.'

'It's not bothering me,' Coulter said. 'I'll come and see you if it does. See you around, Doc.'

He took his leave and walked along the street to the edge of town to collect his horse. He led the animal towards the law office and tethered it to a rail outside a gun shop that was a few yards from the jail, afterwards going back to the livery barn to enter the gloomy interior. A lantern was suspended from a hook over the wide door and, by its dim light Coulter located Julie's horse and saddled the animal. He led it along the street to where he had left his mount.

Coulter liked the feeling of remoteness that gripped him as he looked around the deserted street. He did not know anyone in Peyton Junction, apart from Luke Doyle, and that was the way he liked it. He walked the few yards to the alley beside the law office and stood in its friendly shadows to take stock of the situation. When he peered in through the front window of the office he saw Sheriff Coombe still seated at his desk, and the thin-faced deputy was standing beside the desk, listening to

66

the sheriff's earnest talking.

Acting upon an impulse, Coulter returned to the livery barn. He needed a diversion, something that would hold the attention of the townsfolk while he busted Julie out of her cell. He looked in the small office in the barn and was relieved to find it deserted. There were a dozen or so horses in the barn and he turned them loose and shooed them out back into a big corral before climbing a ladder into the hayloft. He set fire to a pile of hay before departing quickly for the alley beside the jail, and waited out the fleeting moments it took the fire to catch, all the time hoping that some townsman would spot the growing conflagration and raise the alarm before the flames got out of control.

Minutes later, a strident voice shattered the silence.

'Fire! Fire! The stable is burning!'

A man appeared along the sidewalk and came running by Coulter's position in the alley to open the door of the law office. He hurried inside, his voice yelling the word that all western townsfolk feared.

'Fire, Sheriff. There's smoke coming out of the Dentons' barn.'

Coulter craned forward to look into the office. Coombe was sitting immobile in his seat, his big face showing disbelief and his mouth agape. The man raising the alarm shouted the warning again before turning to run back to the street. He retraced his steps along the sidewalk towards the livery barn, followed a few moments later by the lumbering figure of the sheriff. Other voices took up the cry, echoing in the darkness, and men poured out of the saloon and followed the stream of anxious humanity making for the stable.

Coulter stepped out of the alley and looked towards the stable. He could see smoke billowing up out of the hayloft and drifting quickly on the strong breeze. A dull red glow showed in the open doorway of the loft overlooking the street. Excited voices were yelling as men raced to the livery barn, intent on saving the town from destruction.

Coulter drew his pistol and cocked it. He walked to the door of the law office, putting his gun hand behind his back when he saw the small deputy standing in the doorway looking towards the stable. He produced the big gun when he confronted the man. The deputy started back, reaching instinctively for the butt of his holstered pistol until he saw Coulter's gun and then staying the movement.

'Get inside with your hands up,' Coulter said briskly, snatching the man's pistol from its holster.

The deputy moved backward as Coulter crowded him, raising his hands shoulder high, his eyes filled with shock. He shook his head as if he could not believe what was happening. Coulter crossed the threshold and closed the street door with his heel, following the deputy closely, the muzzle of his gun poking the man in the chest.

'Open the cells,' Coulter rasped. 'I want Julie Wade out of there, but quick.'

'Anything you say, mister.' The deputy snatched up a bunch of keys from a corner of the desk and hurried to a door set in the back wall of the office. 'I don't like the idea of holding a woman. Take her out of here. I'll be pleased to see her go.'

They went into the cell block, where a single lantern cast a dim glow through the cells. Julie was seated on a bunk in the nearest cell, her shoulders bowed and her chin sunk on her breast. She looked up at their entrance, and Coulter was pleased by the smile of relief that chased away her grim expression. She got to her feet and picked up her hat as the deputy unlocked the cell door.

Coulter thrust the deputy into the cell as Julie emerged from it, and locked the door.

'Don't make a sound for at least ten minutes or I'll come back and gut-shoot you,' he warned, and the deputy nodded emphatically.

Julie hurried into the main office and crossed to the street door. Coulter paused only to lock the connecting door between the office and the cells and, as he turned to follow the girl, the street door was opened and Sheriff Coombe appeared in the doorway. The big lawman confronted Julie, and both were surprised, but the sheriff acted with surprising speed. He reached for his holstered pistol, and Coulter responded by producing his .45 from the waist band of his trousers . . .

4

Sheriff Coombe was fast. His pistol cleared leather with commendable speed, but, as his big right thumb eared back the hammer, he saw Coulter's gun levelled at him, already cocked, and uttered a groan of disbelief as he opened his hand and allowed his pistol to fall to the floor.

'You got sense,' Coulter declared. 'Come in and shut the door, Sheriff.'

He tossed the bunch of keys to the big lawman and, without being ordered, Coombe walked to the door leading into the cell block and unlocked it. The sheriff opened a cell, entered without comment, and sat down on the bunk as Coulter locked the iron-barred door.

'My guess is that you're one of the two train robbers who escaped the gun trap at the rail depot last week,' Coombe said in a voice that sounded as

72

if it came up from his boots.

'Keep quiet,' Coulter responded. He half-turned to leave but caught a swift movement from the sheriff and swung back, his gun lifting.

Coombe was reaching into a back pocket, and Coulter caught the glint of lamplight on metal. The sheriff pulled a short-barrelled pistol into view, his fleshy face set in stark desperation. Coulter clenched his teeth and lifted his thumb from the hammer of his six-gun. The big weapon blasted echoingly and gun smoke flew in a dark cloud. Coombe took the slug in his upper chest and was knocked sideways by the force of the impact. He fell off the bunk and writhed on the floor.

Coulter cursed soundly as he returned to the front office. Julie was standing by the door, which she had closed. Coulter crossed to her side, opened the door and peered out at the street. There was a lot of activity down around the stable, and he could see flames leaping up through the roof of the building. A figure moved in the shadows on the sidewalk and Coulter drew back in alarm. He pushed the door to as the figure came closer.

'Hey, Sheriff,' a voice called.

Coulter opened the door again. The man outside crowded forward into the doorway. Coulter was back on the threshold, his gun hand down at his side. The newcomer was gripping the butt of his holstered gun, his expression revealing suspicion. Coulter caught his breath as recognition struck him.

'Doyle!' His voice was raised a couple of notches in surprise.

'Coulter!' Doyle's gun hand moved fast, his clawing fingers clutching and lifting the big six-gun holstered on his right thigh, but his instinctive reaction had him twisting and turning away instead of fighting.

Coulter swung up his gun hand, trigger finger tightening. Doyle was moving to the right, blundering back out of the doorway. Coulter's pistol exploded and a lance of orange flame speared from the muzzle. Doyle was moving fast. Coulter swung his pistol as his first slug tore a six-inch sliver of wood from the door post just behind Doyle. He fired again, sending his shot through the wall, judging Doyle's progress. He stepped to his left and his shoulder struck the half-open street door. Searing pain flared through his wound. The shock pulled him up short and he stifled a groan. When he forced himself to go on he blundered through the doorway to the sidewalk, gun swinging. There he paused, breathing heavily. Doyle was out of sight, and the sound of receding footsteps sounded in the alley beside the office.

'Let's go,' Coulter said harshly, struggling against disappointment. He turned to Julie, who had followed him out to the sidewalk. 'I've got our horses at a hitch rail just along there.'

'You fired a shot in the cells!' Julie demanded. 'Did you kill Coombe?'

'The sheriff pulled a hideout gun out of his back pocket,' Coulter replied tersely. 'I hit him high in the chest.'

'I hope he's dead!' Deadly venom sounded in Julie's voice.

Coulter nodded. Julie preceded him along the sidewalk. Coulter pointed to where their horses were tethered. Shadowy figures ran by, attracted by the fire at the livery barn. Coulter waited until Julie was in her saddle before mounting the bay. The girl led the way across the street to enter an alley opposite. Coulter was content to follow her, for she knew the town better than he.

Their hoofs rattled the hard-packed ground in the alley. Coulter glanced back, saw nothing to cause alarm, and heaved a sigh of relief when they cleared the alley and rode across the back lots. Moments later they were well clear of Peyton Junction, and Julie changed direction and led him into the anonymous cover of the night.

Coulter gritted his teeth against flaring pain, and was hard put to remain upright in the saddle as the bay galloped over rough ground. He cursed himself for missing Doyle, and regretted that he didn't have the time to run down the renegade, but consoled himself with the knowledge that there would be another opportunity later.

They rode without talking until Julie reined in to spell the horses. She slid out of the saddle and trailed her reins. Coulter stepped down from the torturous saddle, his body protesting at the demands he had made upon it. His left shoulder was painful, and no matter in which position he held his left arm there was no relief from the nagging ache that suffused the limb. Agony gripped the entire arm, even down to his fingertips.

'How are you feeling?' Anxiety laced Julie's low tone.

'I'm doing fine,' he lied, and told her of his activities around town.

She uttered an exclamation when he mentioned calling on Doc Tracey.

'So you know what happened to me when I shot Henderson,' she said.

'That was a fool thing to do,' he chided. He paused, considered, and then said: 'But I guess I would have done the same thing if I'd been in your boots.'

'But I didn't kill him! There wasn't time to aim properly.' She sighed heavily. 'I won't make that mistake next time.'

'It would have been better to hold your fire until you got him alone somewhere on the range so you could do a good job on him.'

'I didn't have a choice. Henderson pulled his gun the minute he saw me. I thought he was gonna shoot me right there in front of Doc and the sheriff.'

'So he's declared war on you. I guess that makes it easier for us. We know where we stand now.'

'It was a foolish thing you did, busting me out of jail like that. The sheriff saw you. Now he knows what you look like. I pray he's dead.'

'I don't think he is. I had a lot of flesh to aim at. I heard one good bit of news from Doc. He said Al Billing, who rode with the gang, got away when I did.'

'What are you going to do now?' Julie's face was just a pale blur in the soft darkness as she looked at Coulter.

'Take it as it comes.' He shrugged. 'We need to find some good cover because there'll be a big posse out come daylight. You know where we are right now, huh?'

'Sure. We're about halfway to a place where you'll be able to rest up, but we'll give you a spell here because I want to ride into Charlie Morgan's spread around sun-up. Charlie will give us provisions. He hates Henderson as much as I do; his son Billy was shot by two of Henderson's riders about five months ago. It was a callous murder, but Coombe smoothed it over. Charlie hasn't got over Billy's death, and he's living for the day when he can shoot Henderson. I do believe Charlie is mentally unbalanced by what happened to Billy.'

'So Henderson has been making big tracks around the range, huh?' Coulter nodded. 'I guess he's got it coming to him one way or another.'

He took his bedroll from his cantle and spread it on the grass.

'You'd better get some rest,' he advised. 'It'll be tough to keep ahead of the posse that'll be out looking for us.'

'Most of Henderson's hardcases will join the hunt for us,' Julie rejoined. 'Henderson wants me dead now, and Coombe will back him all the way.'

'The sheriff has got something else on his mind right now,' Coulter responded with a harsh chuckle.

He settled down on his right side, trying to ease his left shoulder. Pain nagged his wound but tiredness soon overcame him and he fell asleep despite his discomfort. The sun was rising when he opened his eyes again, and he viewed the new day with dark foreboding.

The smell of coffee wafted across his nostrils as he sat up to find Julie crouching over a small camp-fire. Her face was pale and taut, showing strain in every line of countenance, but she smiled wanly when he arose, and poured hot coffee into a tin mug for him.

'I didn't get the chance to buy supplies or cartridges in town yesterday,' she said. 'We'll just have to tighten our belts until we get to the Morgan place.'

'I'm used to riding hungry.' He took the mug from her, sipped the scalding liquid, and grunted his satisfaction. 'This sure tastes good,' he declared. 'Do you think we'll get help from Morgan?'

'There are some small ranchers around who have felt the weight of Henderson's hand, and they'll look out for us.' Julie paused, steaming mug to her lips, her sharp gaze unwavering. 'We'd better not let anyone know you were with the gang that got shot up last week. It might be better to say you took a job with us a couple of days before Henderson's bunch killed Grandpa.'

'I'll go along with that,' Coulter agreed.

They broke camp and rode on. Coulter's shoulder was even more troublesome than the day before, and he realized that he was doing too much too soon, but he had to keep moving, and suffered his discomfort in silence.

Two hours later they sighted Morgan's spread — a cabin standing beside a stream. There was a small barn and a corral with two horses in it — a shoe-string cattle ranch. As they rode in a tall, thin man appeared in the doorway of the cabin holding a rifle in his hands. The muzzle covered them as they approached.

'That's Charlie Morgan,' Julie said. 'He's always talked of fighting Henderson and his bunch, but he's got enough sense to know he can't win a one-man war.'

Morgan was in his fifties, his weathered face mostly covered by a greying beard. His eyes were dark, filled with a haunted expression, and his smile of welcome, when he recognised Julie, was more like the snarl of a wild animal at bay. He set down his rifle against a door post and came forward quickly.

'Julie, I heard about Henry,' Morgan said in a hard voice. 'I told him enough times to be on his guard. I could see what was coming, but no one would listen to me, not even after Billy was gunned down.' His dark, half-wild gaze, filled with suspicion, flickered to Coulter. 'Who's this?'

'Jack Smith.' Julie threw Coulter a warning glance. 'He rode into our place a few days ago, looking for a job, and Grandpa took him on. Jack helped to fight off Henderson's gunnies when they showed up. I was in town yesterday to talk to the sheriff when Henderson showed up. He pulled a gun on me, Charlie, but I managed to wing him.'

'The hell you say! I wish I'd been there.' Morgan chuckled, and Coulter got the feeling that the man was half-crazed by the death of his son. 'So you're on the run, huh? And you're riding light. Is there anything I can do for you? I'll help any way I can.'

'We need supplies,' Julie said. 'I went into town to stock up but Coombe threw me in jail. Jack busted me out last night, and put a slug in Coombe.'

Morgan nodded emphatically. 'I sure wish I'd been there to see that. There are men around here who would throw in with us if we went up against Henderson's bunch.' He paused, his dark eyes glittering. 'Is Coombe dead?'

'No.' Julie spoke fiercely. 'He would be if I'd fired the shot that downed him.'

'Then 'light and come into the cabin. Ellie will get you some food. Later, we can talk about hitting Henderson where it'll hurt him most. I'll call Benny in shortly. He can ride to fetch in our friends. We'll raid Henderson tonight and pay him back for the trouble he's been causing. I knew the chance would come if I waited long enough.' Morgan laughed, and Coulter, stepping down from his saddle, frowned as he caught a trace of wildness in the sound.

'Hold hard for a moment, Charlie.' Julie spoke cautiously, catching Coulter's expression. 'We can't go up against Henderson openly. He'd wipe us out in a stand-up fight. I kept telling Grandpa to pull in his horns but he wouldn't listen, and now he's dead. Coming out into the open right now would be playing into Henderson's hands. We've got to get a whole lot smarter than we are at the moment to win this fight.'

Coulter mentally agreed. He looked around the little spread, and decided that he and Julie would pull out as soon as possible. He did not want to get caught up in Morgan's desperate plan to fight a range war. Julie had it about right when she said they had to fight smart or die.

A woman appeared in the doorway of the cabin. She was tall, thin; looked very old, but Coulter estimated that she was in her middle fifties. Julie went to her and they embraced. The woman drew Julie into the cabin. Morgan asked questions about the attack on the Mallen spread and Coulter gave terse details. Morgan nodded.

'That's how I figured Henderson would handle it. He's a killer, and now he's started murdering there'll be no holding him.' He threw a glance around to check his surroundings. 'I wouldn't be surprised to see his bunch come riding in here next. I sure made a lot of noise about standing up to him. You say several of Henderson's crew were shot down when they hit Henry? And then you killed two more! Heck, that's almost a third of his outfit! Henderson can't afford to lose men like that. He'll mebbe have a different slant on the business after this. You must be hell on wheels with a gun, Smith. Lucky for Julie you were around when the trouble started.'

Coulter entered the cabin to find Julie and Mrs Morgan cooking food, the smell of which tantalized Coulter's nostrils. He sat down to rest, but felt on edge, and moved his chair so that he could look out a window facing the little yard. He saw Charlie Morgan cross the yard, and a tall, thin young man emerged from the barn to talk to the older man.

'That's my younger son Benny,' said Mrs Morgan, coming to the window and peering out across the yard. 'He took it real hard when Billy was shot dead. I had my work cut out to talk him out of taking up a gun and going for Henderson. Charlie has been breathing fire and brimstone, and that don't help none. Now Henry Mallen is dead, murdered just like Charlie said it would happen, and I fear for the future. When this kind of thing starts there's no telling how it will end. Usually, there's no one left alive.'

Coulter stiffened in his seat when he caught a movement out on the range. He blinked and leaned forward to peer through the window. A rider was jogging down a slope and heading for the cabin. He got to his feet and drew his pistol to check it.

'Rider coming,' he warned.

Julie ran to the window and peered out. Charlie Morgan was coming back to the house with rapid strides to pick up the Winchester propped against the door post. Coulter went outside and Morgan turned to him.

'Wait inside out of sight,' he suggested. 'There's only one man coming, and I can brace him.'

'There may be more waiting just out of sight,' Coulter said tersely. He spun the cylinder of his pistol and then stuck the weapon in his waistband. His shoulder was aching but he ignored the pain. He went to his bay, took his cartridge belt from the bedroll and buckled it around his waist before sliding the pistol into the holster.

The rider came in steadily, looking neither left nor right. The horse was moving at a canter.

'It's Rudi Krantz,' Morgan said suddenly. 'He runs a small spread off to the north. The last time I saw him he said most of his stock had been rustled. No need to ask who stole his beef. It had to be Henderson's outfit.'

The rider came into the yard and reined up in front of Morgan. He was short and wide-shouldered, with powerful arms and large hands. He was old, his face wrinkled, eyes ageless, and white hair showed under the wide brim of his hat. He looked around uneasily.

'Howdy, Charlie,' he greeted. 'I'm glad to see you on your guard. Pete Brister was shot dead in my yard this morning at sun up. Killed by someone who didn't show his face. I'm on my way to town to talk to Coombe, but I know it'll be a waste of time because that fat slob won't do a damn thing about it. I reckon it's time we took a hand ourselves, before anybody else gets killed. I'm ready to go along with you, Charlie, any time you want to call the shots. It may be too late now to win, but we sure as hell got to try.'

'Better late than never, Rudi. In fact, you're just in time. We're about to make a plan to hit Henderson hard. How many guns do you think we can round up?'

'Not enough to do any good, I reckon.' Krantz frowned and scratched his chin. 'If we nail Henderson first off then his outfit might quit. Them gunnies don't fight without pay.'

'This is Jack Smith,' Morgan introduced Coulter. 'Hired on with Henry Mallen and they nailed six of Henderson's outfit before Henry was killed. Smith is a real Heller. He shot Sheriff Coombe in the town jail last night.'

'The hell you say!' Krantz was impressed.

Julie called Coulter from the doorway of the cabin and he went to her.

'Food is ready.' Julie glanced outside at Morgan and Krantz. 'I think we should get out of here soon as we can,' she added in an undertone. 'We don't need hot-heads joining us.'

'That's what I was thinking.' Coulter nodded as he followed the girl into the cabin.

They ate quickly, and Morgan entered the cabin as they were finishing the meal. Ellie Morgan was putting provisions into a sack. Coulter took twenty dollars from his wad of notes and held them out to Morgan, who shook his head emphatically.

'Take it,' Coulter insisted, thrusting the notes at Morgan. 'You'll need to stock up on cartridges at least. It takes a lot to fight a war. And take some advice from someone who knows. Don't go off halfcocked. You'll get wiped out if you do. You've got to fight smart.'

'You're not gonna hit Henderson tonight?' Morgan sounded disappointed.

'I'm not fit to fight openly,' Coulter replied. 'I've got a shoulder wound that hasn't healed up yet and I need to rest it before helling around. We're gonna lie low for a spell, and when I feel ready we'll come back. I suggest you hold your horses for a week or so. Then we'll take on Henderson.'

'There's no time like the present,'

Morgan said doggedly, his eyes filled with an unholy expression. 'I wanta stop Henderson from breathing good fresh air. Billy has been dead nearly six months, and he won't rest until Henderson is buried.'

'It won't do anyone any good if you get yourself killed.' Coulter picked up the gunny sack Ellie Morgan had filled. 'We'll be riding back this way later. Load up with ammunition and stores and be ready to ride when we show.'

Morgan shook his head, only half-convinced by Coulter's common sense.

'Hey, Pa.' Benny Morgan's sharp voice called from outside the cabin. 'There's a bunch of riders coming over the rise and they look like they're loaded for bear.'

Coulter ran to the window, peered out, and saw five riders coming at a gallop towards the cabin. They were still several hundred yards off. He glanced at Julie.

'We'd better make ourselves scarce,' he warned. 'They can only mean trouble. Let's ride before we're spotted.'

They hurried outside. Coulter tied the gunny sack to his cantle. His eyes were narrow slits as he gauged the speed of the approaching riders. Julie grasped her reins and led her horse towards the rear of the cabin.

'Don't mount up yet,' she called to Coulter, who nodded and followed her.

'We'll cover you if they look like they wanta fight,' Morgan called after them.

Coulter shook his head, aware that nothing he said had got through Morgan's head. The man could think of nothing beyond the fact that his son had been killed, and Coulter did not blame him.

With the cabin between them and the approaching riders, Julie swung into her saddle. Coulter followed suit, grunting as pain stabbed through his tender shoulder. They rode out fast, keeping the bulk of the cabin between them and the rapidly approaching newcomers. Julie led the way into a narrow draw that led through rising ground and they dropped out of sight of the cabin and kept moving fast.

Minutes later, Coulter's keen ears picked up the sound of gunfire and he reined in quickly.

'They've got trouble at the cabin,' he called.

Julie twisted in her saddle. 'We'd better keep going,' she decided. 'Charlie will hold them off like he promised. We've got to get clear.'

She rode on and Coulter followed, his ears keened for more shooting. When he heard rapid firing he reined in again and looked back. They had reached higher ground but could not see the Morgan cabin.

'We can't run out on Morgan.' he said worriedly. 'Look, there's smoke in the sky! They've fired the cabin, and Mrs Morgan is there. We've got to fight.'

Julie saw the black tendrils of smoke rising and nodded tensely, her eyes narrowed. She swung her horse and rode back along the draw, pulling her rifle from its scabbard as she did so. Coulter drew his pistol and followed closely. There was a time to run and a time to fight, and he had no illusions about what they had to do right now.

5

A burst of rapid shooting threw harsh echoes across the range as Julie rode out of the draw behind the cabin. Coulter, close behind her, saw two men standing in the open, their horses close by, firing into the back of the little building, which was burning. Smoke was gushing up through the roof. There was more shooting coming from out front.

Julie reined in and slid from her saddle, gripping her rifle. She lifted the weapon and triggered it. Her first shot narrowly missed the nearest of the two men and he swung around quickly.

The girl fired again, this time aiming her shot carefully, and the man staggered and dropped to his knees, hit in the chest. Coulter swung aside from behind the girl, pistol in his hand. He lifted the weapon and fired in a single movement, hardly seeming to aim. The second man, looking around at the sound of shooting coming from his rear, whirled and began to swing his pistol toward Coulter, who fired again. Blood spurted from the man's throat, his gun flipped out of his suddenly nerveless hand, and he followed the weapon down into the dust.

Coulter turned his gun on the man Julie had fired at, who was on his knees with his left hand pressed against the ground for support. Blood was spreading across the front of his shirt. He was trying desperately to bring his pistol into play. Gun smoke drifted into Coulter's face as he fired, and he grunted with satisfaction when the man fell back and lay still. Coulter ran to the back of the cabin and hurried along to the right-hand rear corner. Shooting was hammering out front as he ran along the side of the building and peered out across the yard.

Two men were down in cover, shooting rapidly into the cabin. A third man was stretched out inertly nearby. Coulter opened fire, and when his slugs smacked the ground around the two men they stopped shooting and ducked out of sight. Smoke from the cabin was drifting across the yard.

Coulter moved out into the open. His blue eyes were narrowed as he went in for the kill. One of the men rose up to look around. Coulter fired instantly. The man dropped back into cover, his gun falling from his hand, and the surviving raider jumped to his feet and ran swiftly towards the barn. A rifle in the house blasted a single shot and the man went down in a sprawling fall. He pushed his face into the dust and slumped while gun echoes faded and lost themselves in the illimitable space of the prairie.

Coulter released his pent-up breath in a long sigh, his keen gaze sweeping his surroundings. Nothing moved out there on the range. He paused to reload his pistol. Charlie Morgan was ushering his wife out of the burning cabin and his son, Benny, followed closely, dragging an inert Krantz by the scruff of the neck. Coulter frowned. Krantz looked like he was dead.

Julie went to Ellie Morgan's side, but the woman turned and ran back into the burning cabin.

'Come on,' she called. 'Let's save what we can.'

'Forget it,' Charlie Morgan yelled. 'We've got to get out of here. Benny, saddle up the horses. Ellie, grab provisions, and that's all.'

'Who are these men?' Coulter asked. 'Was it a posse?'

'No.' Morgan's face was ghastly, his eyes flaring with emotion. 'Henderson wouldn't send in a posse to do this kind of work. These are some of his gunnies come to murder and burn us out. You heard what Krantz said when he rode in. One of his men was shot dead at his place this morning by a sniper. Now Krantz is dead, and we know who shot him, so we've got to hit back.'

Julie walked out to where the dead attackers lay sprawled in the dust. She looked at two of them and then came back to where Coulter was standing. Her eyes were narrowed, filled with shock, and her lips moved stiffly when she spoke.

'Curly Brogan is dead out there,' she reported, 'and so is Jed Stone. They rode for Henderson. So what do we do now? You can bet that Coombe will cover for Henderson. He did nothing about Henderson's men killing Grandpa, and don't forget that I was the one Coombe put behind bars, not Henderson.'

Coulter looked around. Ellie Morgan was emerging from the cabin, carrying a sack of supplies. Benny Morgan was saddling horses at the corral. The crackling of the burning building was loud in the surrounding silence and smoke billowed up into the clear sky. It seemed to Coulter that time itself stood still, and he was aware that he had to make the decision about what they should do next. He moved his left shoulder experimentally and the pain that struck him warned that the only thing he could do was rest up until his wound had fully healed.

'I'll tell you what I'm gonna do.' Charlie Morgan spoke harshly, his voice trembling with emotion. 'I'm gonna ride into town with these dead killers and show them to the folk there. Coombe can't cover for Henderson any longer. The law has got to do something. Henderson has gone too far this time, and honest folk will want to see justice done.'

'I wouldn't count on that, Charlie,' Julie warned. 'Coombe is in this too deep to stop now. Ride into town and they'll skin you alive.' She glanced at Coulter, and, when he remained silent, she said: 'We're not interested in a stand-up fight. We know we couldn't win it nohow. We must play a waiting game. It's the only way.'

'Thanks for helping out just now,' Morgan said, and his tone made it plain that he would not budge from his decision. 'We're going to town. I hope you'll make out, Julie. It's no life for a woman, fighting on the run. Coombe will send out a posse after you, and if you shoot at them you'll put yourself outside the law.'

'We'll take our chances.' Julie was thin-lipped. 'If the law won't do what's right then we have to handle it ourselves. There's no other way. We don't have a choice.'

'Strip these raiders of anything you might need,' Morgan said. 'Take their guns and cartridges. You'll sure need lots of everything before you're done.'

Coulter went around the dead men removing their gunbelts and searching their saddle-bags for ammunition. By the time he and Julie rode out again, Morgan was leading his grim cavalcade towards the distant town and the cabin was burning itself into a heap of smoking ashes.

Julie rode ahead of Coulter up the draw, and she remained silent until they reached the top and emerged on higher ground. They dismounted to rest the horses. Coulter looked back over the range. The still-smoking cabin was far below. There was no movement anywhere on the range. Coulter sat down on a large boulder and tried to relax. Julie busied herself lighting a small fire to prepare coffee.

'I don't cotton to this business,' Coulter said quietly, 'and the more I think about it the less I like it. There's no way you can win, Julie. You've put yourself outside the law already, and a posse will be scouring the country for you. Honest folk will be afraid to help you. If you heed my advice you'll shake the dust of this range off your feet and head for pastures where you're not known. If you leave now you might get away with it and manage to start afresh somewhere else.'

'I'm aware of the odds.' Julie handed him a mug of coffee and he murmured his thanks. 'I don't care what happens to me as long as I can kill Henderson.

I want to see him dead before I'll be satisfied.'

'I understand how you feel right now.' Coulter studied her set face and could judge the full extent of her shock and grief. 'But you don't have to do a blame thing about Henderson, and it shouldn't matter to you how he dies so long as he winds up on Boot Hill so pull out and lose yourself somewhere while I kill Henderson for you.'

He watched her face for reaction, saw nothing but determination, and sighed. 'Give me another week to rest up and then I'll ride into town and put a slug through Henderson when I kill Doyle. Then all your troubles will be over. You could settle down and pick up the pieces of your life. I'm gonna kill Luke Doyle, so taking Henderson out will be no big deal. I'm slated for Boot Hill anyway. It doesn't matter one way or the other what I do, and if they get me I'll take your problems with me.'

'I can't let you do that.' She shook her head emphatically. 'I appreciate your offer, but killing Henderson is something I've got to do. I couldn't live with myself if I ran out now.'

'It wouldn't be running out,' he insisted. 'I'm in this anyway, whether I like it or not. Henderson's men have been shooting at me, and I will go on with it until it's done.'

'Let's ride on,' she suggested. 'We can talk some more about this later. You're looking pale and worn out. You need to rest up. If you're not careful you're going to run yourself into the ground.'

Coulter grinned. 'I'll go along with that for now, the way I'm feeling. Where are we heading?'

'I'm making for a cabin that Grandpa built on the north edge of our range for when we were out that way. We used to spend our time equally between the two cabins, and I don't think Henderson's bunch is aware of it. We should be safe there for a week at least.'

They mounted up and rode on. Coulter became weary as the hours passed. By the time he sighted a cabin half hidden in dense undergrowth he was reeling in his saddle. Dismounting, he almost fell to his knees, and Julie hurried to his side and supported him as he staggered into the cabin. He sprawled face down on a bunk and lay as if dead while the girl busied herself with moving in.

Coulter slept, and night had fallen when he reopened his eyes. The dim light of a lantern relieved the darkness, and the appetizing smell of cooking food assailed his nostrils to torment his hunger. He sat up carefully and began to take notice of his surroundings. His shoulder was stiff and painful, and he grunted when he moved it gingerly.

Julie came to his side. She looked rested and less shocked now, and smiled wryly at him as he got to his feet.

'You've had a long sleep,' she observed. 'How are you feeling now?'

'Much better, thanks. I sure was scraping the bottom of the barrel when we got here.'

'Come and eat, and then I'll take a look at your shoulder. If you rest up for three days you should be out of the wood as far as complications go.'

Coulter agreed, and after they had eaten he removed his shirt. Julie's fingers were cool upon his shoulder as she treated his wound.

'It hasn't opened up again,' she reported, 'and looks to be healing nicely, although it is still puffy and red. Rest up until the soreness goes and you should be able to forget about it.'

Julie applied a clean bandage to the wound, and Coulter felt easier when he was lying down again. Darkness pressed against the small panes of the window. He considered the miles they had travelled since parting from Charlie Morgan and wondered how the rancher had fared when he reached Peyton Junction. He did not expect Charlie to find justice . . .

Four days passed interminably. Coulter rested, and eventually grew tired of sitting or lying around, but was aware there was no other way of recovering. Time had to work its magic on his body. He whiled away the hours cleaning his guns and considering the situation. As the days passed he became set on the idea of getting Julie to pull out while he handled the situation, but when he broached the subject to the girl he found her adamant in her decision to kill Henderson, and no amount of argument could sway her from that purpose.

'Would you allow me to shoot Doyle for you?' she countered, gazing at him with deadly intention in her narrowed eyes.

Coulter shook his head.

'I'm thinking of riding to town in the morning,' he said. 'We'll call at Charlie Morgan's place on the way and find out how he got on.'

'Are you sure you're OK now? A few more days won't make any difference. Don't move out too soon or you'll undo all the good work I've put in on that wound.'

'I'm itching to hit the trail,' he responded. 'I can't rest while Luke Doyle is still breathing. I need to see him dead before I can get on with my life.'

'That's exactly how I feel about Henderson.' Julie smiled knowingly, and Coulter could imagine the turmoil seething in her mind.

They were almost out of provisions when they set out in the direction of Peyton Junction, and a day in the saddle brought them within sight of Morgan's place. The cabin was just a heap of ashes, and the stench of the fire hung over the area like a poisonous cloud. There was no sign of Charlie Morgan or his family. Coulter scouted around while Julie sat her mount in the yard. He found fresh tracks of two animals coming into and leaving the yard, and estimated that they had been made at least twenty-four hours earlier. His face was expressionless when he rejoined Julie and acquainted her with the news.

'What do you think happened to Charlie when he reached town?' Julie asked.

'I should think he and Benny were jailed; probably Ellie as well. Charlie made a wrong move by riding in to report.' Coulter shrugged. 'I guess there's only one way to find out for sure. We'll ride in after dark and scout around.'

They continued, and Coulter was congratulating himself on feeling much better despite spending hours in the saddle when Julie called a warning and he looked around quickly to see two riders coming over a rise to their left. The riders swung in their direction. Coulter frowned. They had been seen. He dropped his right hand to his side to be ready for action, but Julie gave a cry of relief.

'That's Tom Loman,' she observed. 'He owns the TL spread. He's against Henderson, and that's his foreman, Joe Hayman, with him.'

Coulter relaxed slightly, but kept his

right hand close to the butt of his gun, ready for action. The two riders approached at a canter, and a smile appeared on the face of the older man as they drew closer.

'Julie, I'm glad to see you.' Loman was in his forties, medium-sized and powerful, with wide, heavy shoulders and big hands. He reined in, his pleasure obviously genuine. He glanced at Coulter with narrowed blue eyes, but his attention remained on Julie. 'I was just saying to Joe that we've got to do something about Henderson. Where arc you going? You can't head into town. Coombe has a posse out searching for you, and you'll be arrested the minute you show your face in Peyton Junction. What really happened out at your place? Henderson has put out a story that Henry shot Carson without warning when hc was sent to your place with a message. More men were sent to check out the situation when Carson reported, and they were all shot out of their saddles.'

'That's the kind of story I'd expect from Henderson,' Julie said bitterly.

'When you rode into town you drew on Henderson without warning,' Loman observed, 'and in front of witnesses.'

'At the ranch we were attacked without warning.' Julie's voice trembled with emotion as she recounted the incident. 'This is Jack Smith,' she went on. 'If he hadn't ridden in the day before the attack, looking for a job, Henderson's gunnies would have killed me. I'm riding into town now to finish Henderson.'

'What happened to Charlie Morgan?' Coulter asked. 'We were at his place when he was attacked by a bunch of Henderson's gunnies.'

'He's in jail with Ellie and Benny. Charlie threatened to shoot Henderson on sight. Coombe is nursing a bullet wound, but he's on duty, and he jailed Charlie to be on the safe side. There's a lot of talk around town about Henderson going too far, but no one is gonna do anything about the situation.

Henderson is planning on bringing in more gunnies.' Loman shook his head. 'All the signs are that this will be a full-blown range war. My sympathies are with you, Julie, but a man would be a fool to take your side in this against the odds.'

'Sometimes a man has to stand up and be counted,' Julie replied. 'But I don't blame you, Tom, for turning a blind eye. Henderson is playing for keeps now.'

'If there's anything I can do short of actively resisting Henderson then look me up.' Loman shook his reins and prepared to go on. 'It ain't fitting for a woman to take up a gun. You're heading into bad trouble, Julie.'

Coulter sighed heavily. He grasped Julie's reins and held her horse motionless, his gaze on Loman as the rancher departed.

'You'd be a lot safer with Loman,' he observed. 'Why don't you ride with him and let me get on with what I have to do?'

'That's a nice try,' she responded, 'but no thanks. I've got a date with Jethro Henderson in town and nothing will keep me from it.'

They rode on and the miles slipped by. Shadows were growing long across the range when they sighted Peyton Junction. They dismounted to await full darkness. Silence pressed in around them and Coulter felt a sense of remoteness settle upon him. He did not feel happy about the situation. Julie sat by his side, motionless and silent, and he could sense that she had no wish to converse.

'Time to go,' he said at length. 'We'll ride closer and leave our horses behind Doc Tracey's house. 'I reckon to call on the doc to get the latest news. What do you think?'

'That's a good idea.' Julie climbed into her saddle and started forward through the shadows.

Coulter let the girl lead the way. He remained a couple of yards behind, following her silhouette against the lights of the town until they reined in at the rear of the doctor's house, which was in darkness. They tethered their horses, and Julie led the way around to the front of the house, where two lighted windows welcomed them. Coulter watched the approaches to the house while Julie knocked at the door. The town was silent and still, with few people on the sidewalks.

Doc Tracey answered the door and ushered them inside with the minimum of delay when he recognised Julie.

'I've been wondering where you two were lying low,' he said with a smile.

'What's been happening around town, Doc?' Coulter asked. 'Give us the lowdown.'

'It ain't good for you!' Tracey sighed and expelled his breath in a long sigh, shaking his head as he did so. 'There's a big posse been out for days, searching for you and Julie. They came back this afternoon, and the word is that they'll be riding out again in the morning. Luke Doyle is

115

wearing a deputy sheriff badge now, and he's been leading the posse because he knows you by sight. It seems Coombe described the man who shot him, and Doyle says it's you. They want you bad, son.'

'I can live with that.' Coulter smiled grimly. 'What's Henderson's condition?'

It's a pity Julie's slug didn't put out his light. There was only an inch in it, but that's the way it goes. The Devil is taking care of Jethro Henderson, it looks like. He's sitting up in a bed in the hotel, giving orders and making plans. They say he's got ten more gunnies on his payroll, and he's calling for more. Thad Henderson is running the JH spread at the moment, and, if anything, he's worse than his father.'

'Thad Henderson?' Coulter queried.

'Don't tell me you haven't heard of Thad.' Tracey threw a quick glance at Julie. 'Thad is Jethro's only son, and if I tell you that he's gone around the county wearing twin six-guns strapped around his waist ever since he's been big enough to carry them then you'll get some idea of what he's like. He's trouble with a capital T, and he's been sweating for revenge since Jethro took Julie's bullet. If you happen to come up against Thad and his gunnies then you'd better say your prayers.'

Coulter shook his head. He didn't mind the opposition building up. He would bide his time and strike hard and fast when he was ready, but he did not want Julie at his side when the time for shooting came. He could tell by her expression that she would not change her mind about accompanying him, and tried to think of a reason that would make her reconsider her position. He needed to have all his wits centred upon himself when the showdown came.

'I'd like to take a look around the town to get my bearings,' he said. 'Can Julie stay with you until I get back, Doc?'

'Sure thing. I expect she could do

with a bath and a good supper.'

'You can't get rid of me that easy.' Julie flared instantly.

'It'll be a simple matter for me to float around town on my own,' Coulter argued. 'Don't make life harder than it has to be. I'm not likely to start anything while that posse is in town. When they ride out tomorrow there'll be that many men less to worry about.'

'That sounds like good sense to me,' Tracey agreed.

Julie sighed and shook her head. 'I'm sticking to you like glue,' she responded. 'If there's any shooting to be done then I want in on it.'

Coulter glanced at Tracey, and the doctor shrugged.

'I've known Julie since the day she was born,' he said, 'and even as a child she was obstinate. You're wasting your time trying to dissuade her, son. It's obvious she's made up her mind about killing Henderson, and hell and high water won't stop her.'

'Determination is a good thing,' Coulter observed, 'but only if it is backed by common sense.'

'Two guns are better than one,' Julie said harshly. 'I think we'd better be on the move, Jack.'

Tracey moved to the street door to open it for them, and froze with his hand on the handle as a heavy fist pounded the panel on the outside. He threw a startled glance at Coulter, who had instinctively drawn his pistol.

'Were you seen coming here?' Tracey demanded.

Coulter shook his head.

'You'd better get in the back room until I've checked.' Tracey nudged Julie in the back and the girl walked quickly along the corridor.

Coulter followed her closely. The hammering at the door sounded again. Coulter covered the street door, and watched the doctor open it. He could hear Julie breathing heavily at his side. She was clutching his left sleeve nervously. Tracey's voice boomed out, demanding the business of the visitor, and Coulter heard a mumbling voice reply. He clenched his teeth, struggling against a surge of anger, for the visitor was Luke Doyle . . .

6

'Doc, can you come over to the jail right away?' Luke Doyle demanded, his tone harsh and unfeeling. 'Charlie Morgan hung himself in his cell. We cut him down, but there ain't no sign of life in him.'

Tracey uttered an imprecation, and then said. 'I'll get my bag. See you over at the jail.'

'There's no need to hurry,' Doyle replied. 'I think Morgan's dead.'

The front door was slammed, and Coulter went forward to where the doctor was standing.

'I guess you heard that,' Tracey said. 'There's apparently no end to this trouble, and I'm beginning to think something's got to be done about the way the law is backing Henderson. Doyle is a known outlaw, and yet they've given him a law star.'

'You'll have to talk to the leading men of the town,' Coulter observed. 'The remedy is in their hands, not mine. I'll put Doyle out of it as soon as I can draw a bead on him, but you and the good men of the town will have to handle the sheriff.'

'Stay here until I return.' Tracey sighed heavily and departed.

Julie came to Coulter's side. 'You're sweating,' she observed. 'You wanted to go out and shoot Doyle as soon as you heard his voice.'

Coulter nodded. 'I guess I need some patience. But my time will come.'

'That's the way I feel about Henderson.' Julie's eyes were like creek pebbles, hard and shining. 'So don't try to put me off or drop me by the wayside.'

'Sure. I was merely trying to keep you out of trouble. And about Thad Henderson. You didn't mention him, and you can't leave him out of your reckoning. If you kill the father you'll have to kill the son.'

'I know that.' Julie's face was pale and taut. 'I just wish it was all over.'

'I can understand what you're going through.' He nodded. 'Just relax and it will come to pass. Now will you stay here while I take a look around the town? I want to see what kind of a set-up they've got. I'm pretty safe on my own — there's only Doyle and the sheriff who are likely to recognize me, but everyone in town knows you by sight. You can count on being spotted before you go many yards.'

'Will you promise not to shoot Doyle, if you come across him?' she asked.

'I promise. All I want to do is check on how many men Henderson has around him and how good they are at their job. If I find a blind spot in their defence I'll come back for you and we'll strike at once — together. How does that sound?'

She nodded, her lips compressed against the drag of rampant emotion. 'I'll wait here for you,' she agreed reluctantly, 'but I won't be able to rest until you get back.'

Coulter patted her shoulder and moved off immediately. 'There must be a back door,' he said. 'See me out and then settle down. I shan't be long.'

He departed by the rear door, walked through the gloom to the street, and paused in the dense shadows surrounding a tree. He looked around. There was a crowd of townsfolk standing on the street in front of the law office, some carrying lanterns, and they were making a lot of noise.

A pang of disbelief that Charlie Morgan had killed himself flared in Coulter's mind. The man had been burning with vengeance because of the death of his son, and the last thing he would consider was suicide. So he had been murdered, and probably by Luke Doyle. Coulter could only wonder that Doyle had been given a deputy star, but a crooked sheriff working in cahoots with a range-grabbing rancher would welcome an experienced outlaw to his fold.

Coulter joined the crowd outside the law office and listened to the gossip filtering through the close ranks of curious townsmen. Many were not pleased by the news that Charlie Morgan had hanged himself. There was an undercurrent of resistance to the law running through those present, and more than one man voiced an opinion that it was time the county had a new sheriff.

'I never saw anything like the set-up they got around here,' said a tall, thin man. 'It's obvious Coombe is crooked. Henderson has been running the small ranchers off the range for months, picking on first one and then another and forcing them out. Now Charlie Morgan has died in jail, and they're trying to tell us he hung himself. Well, I knew Charlie for years, and a harder working man I never met. He wasn't the type to kill himself, and for the last six months I never heard him talk of anything but avenging Billy. That's all he lived for, and I reckon that's why he's dead. They killed him in the jail, and you don't have to look any further than Henderson's set-up to find the killer.'

Angry voices agreed with the speaker. Coulter, looking around, spotted two men standing on the edge of the crowd. Both were heavily armed — one of them wearing twin six-guns on crossed cartridge belts. Coulter took a second look at the gun man, who was talking earnestly to his hard-bitten companion, and nudged the man next to him.

'Who's that standing by the buckboard wearing twin guns?' he asked.

The man glanced in the direction Coulter indicated.

'Thad Henderson,' he confirmed, 'and that's Frank Jessop with him. I'm getting out of here. They won't let anyone make a stand against the JH brand. I got a feeling there's gonna be bad trouble. Jethro Henderson was shot a few days ago, and Thad will wanta make an example of whoever did that.'

The man moved off immediately.

Coulter edged towards the sidewalk to the right of the jail, and gained the dense shadows around it. He found an alley-mouth and stepped into its cover. When he looked for Thad Henderson again the man was moving away in the opposite direction, and his companion, Frank Jessop, was shouldering his way into the crowd. Jessop was head and shoulders above most of the townsmen, and although some of them protested at the rough treatment he was dealing out, no one objected when they realized who was pushing them around.

A gun blasted, throwing echoes across the town, and suddenly there was no movement on the street and a heavy silence settled as the echoes of the shot died away. Then the crowd opened outward, fleeing quickly from the scene, leaving Jessop standing alone with a prostrate figure at his feet — the man who had been protesting vociferously. A few seconds later there was no one in view, and Jessop holstered his gun and set off along the street in the direction Thad Henderson had taken.

Coulter was shocked by the casual manner in which a man had been killed. He gazed at the figure lying in the street until his attention was caught by a movement along the sidewalk. He saw Doc Tracey cross to the corpse and drop to his knees to examine it. A moment later the doctor arose and went on in the direction of his home, and Coulter moved swiftly to intercept him. He caught up with Tracey at the doctor's front door.

'Hold it a moment, Doc,' Coulter said, and Tracey swung round. 'I was taking a look around the town and saw the shooting outside the jail. Julie's inside your house. I managed to talk her into staying put until I get back. So what happened to Charlie Morgan? Is he dead?'

'He's certainly dead.' Tracey shook his head. 'There's no argument about that. It's the way he died that's in doubt. I found him with some cord around his neck which was tied to the bars of his cell door. It looked like he hung himself, but the marks around his neck point to a different method of strangulation. Morgan was killed manually — finger marks caused extensive bruising, and they show up quite plainly. Someone went to considerable trouble to murder Morgan and make it look like suicide. Of course, no one is admitting anything, and Luke Doyle is the lowest form of scum I've ever met. He actually threatened to shoot me if I didn't state that Morgan had committed suicide.'

'You don't have to tell me about Doyle. But he ain't got much rope left. I'll drop on to him pretty soon, you can bet, and then he'll be out of it permanently.'

'I shall talk to the members of the town council at their next meeting,' Traccy said, 'and I'll leave them in no uncertainty as to where their civic duty lies. Coombe will have to go, and steps must be taken to curb Jethro Henderson.'

'You'd better be careful, Doc,' Coulter warned. 'It looks like Henderson is playing for big stakes, and he wouldn't let you stand in his way. Keep your lip buttoned on your intention. Doyle is a callous killer, and if you put his back up then you'll be in real trouble. I'm gonna scout around the town now the excitement about Charlie Morgan is over. If I get a chance at Doyle I'll take it with both hands. When I come back I'll knock on your back door. Is that OK by you?'

'Sure. I'll tell Julie to expect you if I'm called out again, which happens all the time in my job.'

Coulter nodded and moved away, keeping to the shadows. He paused under the lone tree and waited until Tracey had disappeared into his house before going on. The street was now devoid of life, and silence pressed in around him.

The body had been removed. Coulter paused in the shadows opposite the law office and looked around. Footsteps sounded along the opposite sidewalk and he picked out a moving figure that paused opposite. Yellow lamplight flared halfway across the street when the office door was opened. A man entered the office, and full darkness swept in again when the door was slammed. Coulter looked left and right. There were lights showing in the big windows of the saloon, and he could hear loud voices emanating from the building. He looked toward the hotel, but decided against visiting it because Henderson would be too strongly guarded for a successful attempt to be made against him.

He crossed the street to the law office, making for the alley beside it, and stepped into its cover to pause and look around. A strong breeze was blowing along the street and he was about to close in on the law office window when he picked up a furtive sound that was half-smothered by the background noise of loose boards rattling. He dropped his hand to the butt of his gun and looked around. A faint movement across the street, coming almost from the spot where he had been standing over there, caught his attention and he narrowed his gaze as he tried to pick out details.

A gun flashed from the opposite shadows, taking Coulter by surprise. He ducked back into the cover of the alley, drawing his gun, and a string of shots split the silence so fast it sounded like a drum roll. His first thought was that he had been spotted and his reaction was to flee, until he realized that the slugs had not been aimed at him. Someone had emptied a pistol into the lighted windows of the law office.

Coulter eased forward to view the street. He heard footsteps running away along the opposite sidewalk, and sudden hope flared in his chest as he wondered if any of the shots had struck either Doyle or Coombe. He realized his position was dangerous and eased back into the alley. He had to lose himself in the darkness before a search was made of the surroundings.

Moving swiftly, he traversed the alley to the back lot, and paused there to consider. He was not being very successful in his attempt to get a shot at Doyle. The townsfolk were too jumpy, and he wondered how he could use their inflammation to further his own cause. He moved silently to his right through the darkness until he reached another alley, and returned by it to the main street. Two figures were standing on the sidewalk in front of the jail, gazing around as if expecting the man with the gun to start shooting again.

It was impossible to identify either of the men, although Coulter was certain Sheriff Coombe was not one of them. He decided to postpone his mission until later, and had turned to fade into deep shadow when a voice spoke to him from his right.

'Coulter, I've been watching you. I've been looking for you for days, and spotted you coming out of the Doc's house earlier.'

Coulter half-turned to see a shadowy figure standing in a doorway, and straying beams of light from an adjacent lantern cast a metallic sheen on the pistol the man was holding. The man showed his teeth in a wide smile and holstered his gun, and Coulter allowed the fine edge of his alertness to slip away.

'Al?' he demanded hesitantly. 'Al Billing?'

'Yeah, it's me. I took a slug in my left arm when I got away from that gun trap at the rail depot, and I've been hanging around in the hope of catching up with you. Were you shot bad?'

'From behind in the left shoulder. I'm sure glad to see you, Al. Why didn't you high tail it out of here?'

'I knew you wouldn't leave.' Billing closed on Coulter. 'I guessed you'd stick around to get Doyle, and I want a piece of that action.'

'Did you shoot into the law office a few minutes ago?' Coulter asked.

Billing chuckled deep in his throat.

'Yeah, I did. I couldn't resist throwing a scare into Doyle, and I wanted him to think you were closing in on him. He's scared of you. He ran me down last week, him and a posse. I expected to die, but Doyle offered me a deal. He fancies being the county sheriff around here, and offered me a hundred dollars to shoot Coombe. He gave me fifty bucks on account, and I said I'd do the job. He wouldn't offer you the same deal though. He wants you dead. You almost plugged him the evening you shot Coombe. Why in hell didn't you kill that crooked sheriff when you had the chance?'

'Doyle knows I'll kill him for setting up the gang,' Coulter said fiercely. 'And I'll go through fire and water to get him.'

'Do you think I wouldn't?' Billing cursed furiously. 'I'll kill Doyle, but I want to bleed some more dough outa him before he bites the dust. Apart from that, I got a deal cooking that might interest you. Jethro Henderson is

135

playing a deep game, and someone winged him last week. I stand to pick up a hundred bucks if I can find the gal who put that slug in him. He doesn't want her dead, just taken prisoner. There's a lot going on around here that might be worth your while to look into, Wayne. The gang is gone, and we'll put Doyle down for that, but we have to make the best of the situation. We can line our pockets around here.'

'Not me.' Coulter spoke harshly. 'I've had a bellyful of that way of life. I'm gonna see Doyle down in the dust before I quit, and when he's dead I'll head for other parts — some place where I ain't known. I'm quitting, Al, and if you've got any sense you'll do the same.'

'That might be right for you,' Billing protested. 'You're a young man, but me; I'm too long in the tooth to make a fresh start. I'm gonna pick up what I can from around here before I think of hauling my freight.'

'It might be better to pull out now,'

Coulter urged. 'I'm against Jethro Henderson and I plan to make life tough for him. I wouldn't want you getting in my way, Al.'

'Have you got something lined up? Hell, I'll come in with you if you need help. What's the pay like?'

'I won't be drawing any pay for what I have in mind. You'd do well to pull stakes now. There's gonna be big trouble here before long, and it looks like you'll be the dog in the manger.'

'If you're going up against Henderson then you've picked a bad one to buck, pal. Did you see that killer Jessop murder the townsman earlier? In front of witnesses, too, and no protest was raised. I reckon you're the one should pull out fast, Wayne.'

'I can't do that. I'm committed.'

'I've got a shack on the edge of town,' Billing said. 'Why don't we go there and talk it over? I'm sure we can come to some agreement about what to do together. There's some easy dough to be made before we kill Doyle.'

'I wouldn't trust Doyle any further than I could throw him. He set us up, Al, and the whole gang was shot to pieces. As far as I'm concerned, Doyle has got to be put down fast.'

'OK, but don't let us lose sight of the main chance. We can screw some dough outa Jethro Henderson. He's spitting mad about the gal that plugged him, and he'll pay through the nose to lay his hands on her. Where did you lie low after that gun trap? You sure covered your tracks. Coombe had two posses out chasing after us, and they nearly got me several times. But Doyle said they never set eyes on you.'

'Listen, Al, and get this straight. I can see that we've settled down on opposite sides of the fence. I was shot bad, much worse than you, and the folk who helped me out were in bad trouble with Henderson. There was a girl and her grandfather, and the old man was murdered in cold blood by Henderson's killers. They would have killed me, too, if I hadn't started throwing lead. So I'm on the side of that girl now, which means shooting at Henderson, and I'm gonna do that any way I can, so you'd better cut your losses and get the hell out before we have to face each other. There's nothing around here for you so get out soon as you can.'

'So it's like that, huh? OK, I can read signs as well as the next man. You've taken up with that gal Henderson wants to get hold of, huh? That's about the weight of it.'

'You're getting hold of the wrong end of the stick, Al. I got caught up in the shooting when Henry Mallen was killed, and it's personal now.'

'That's OK by me, Wayne. We could hire ourselves out to Henderson's opposition and clean up by shooting Henderson. It's all the same to me. I've seen the way the land lies around here. The town council is run by half-a-dozen businessmen who would cough up big for someone to hit the Henderson bunch. I've been with Doyle when he's talked to some of them, and they are ripe for action. Henderson has been pulling tricks that are too close to the line, and he's got to go, but there's no one strong enough to stand up to him.'

'But everyone would know we are two of the outlaws from Blackjack Dawson's gang and wouldn't give us a chance.' Coulter shook his head. 'My way is the only way. It's that or nothing. Cut your losses and pull out, Al. I can't wait to get clear, and I won't stop running until I hit the Canadian border. That's how bad it is.'

'I'm about flat broke, pard, and I won't even think of pulling out until I've lined my pockets. OK, so we are playing on different sides. Well, that can be handled. I won't do anything that might foul you up if you don't cramp my style. We both want the same thing as far as Doyle is concerned, and we can attend to him later but I'd like to milk this situation before you start the killing.'

'I want Doyle dead, but fast,' Coulter

insisted. 'The gang won't rest while he's still breathing.'

'Have you got any dough on you? I know you never threw your cash around like the rest of us. You've been saving your proceeds to buy a ranch, huh? I guess you've got quite a wad stashed away someplace, Wayne. Why don't you make it worth my while to haul my freight? I'm on my uppers. All I need is a stake, and when I get it I'll blow.'

'Sure,' Coulter said immediately. 'I don't have money on me right now. It's cached in Newton, so why don't you ride there and wait for me? I'll give you a hundred bucks when I show up. How does that sound?

'Suits me. If you knock off Doyle then I got nothing to hang around here for. I got fifty bucks from Doyle, and that'll keep me until you show up in Newton. I'll be hanging out in Dan Remo's saloon. We had some good times there, pard. I'll get my gear together and head out in the morning. Will that suit you?'

'It'll be fine.' Coulter nodded.

'Good luck, then. I'll be waiting for you in Newton.' Billing stuck out his right hand and Coulter gripped it. 'I'm sure glad I saw you tonight, pard. I didn't want to get involved in this crooked deal. It smells to high heaven. There's a lot in it that don't appeal. You better watch your step, Wayne, or you might finish up losing out. They're playing for high stakes around here.'

'I can handle it,' Coulter said.

'Play your cards close to your vest, pard.' Billing turned abruptly and faded into the shadows.

Coulter stood motionless in the blackness of the sidewalk for long moments after Billing disappeared, his thoughts racing. He would pay Billing off, if the man departed for Newton without getting involved in the local situation. He thought of Luke Doyle, and started walking along the sidewalk towards the law office. There was no time like the present to tie up loose ends, and Doyle was living on borrowed time.

The silence hanging over the town was broken by several shots being fired, and Coulter moved into an alley and stood listening intently, his gun in his right hand. He counted four shots, and listened to the echoes fading slowly into the distance. No slugs came his way, for which he was thankful, and he wondered at the significance of the action. He was about to close in on the law office when voices sounded across the street and he spotted three figures emerging from the shadows to start across to the hotel.

Coulter frowned, for one of the figures was obviously a woman, and she was struggling against the grip of one of the men with her. Her angry voice came quite plainly to Coulter, and he stared in shock at the fast-moving trio. The woman was Julie, and she was a prisoner.

7

Coulter went along the sidewalk on tip-toes, intending to cut off the trio before they reached the hotel, but his quarry gained the sidewalk ahead of him and disappeared into the well-lit lobby before he could get within striking distance. He holstered his gun and followed closely, pausing in the doorway of the hotel to look around. He was in time to see Julie being bundled into a room on the left.

A clerk was seated at the reception desk, and took no notice of the trio, although Julie was protesting loudly. Coulter entered the lobby and hurried to the door of the room into which Julie had been taken. The clerk jumped up from the desk when he saw Coulter, and protested vociferously as he came forward. Coulter opened the door with his left hand and snaked his pistol from its holster as he crossed the threshold into a large room.

The two men were in the act of tying Julie to a chair. The girl, although struggling energetically, was unable to break free. One of the men slapped her face as Coulter slammed the door. Julie stopped struggling and looked up, her expression showing desperation, and her eyes filled with immeasurable relief at the sight of Coulter with drawn gun. The two men swung around simultaneously, and both froze at the sight of Coulter covering them.

'What's going on?' Coulter demanded.

'They came into the doc's house,' Julie said instantly. 'They shot Doc Tracey in cold blood when he tried to resist them, and brought me here. They are two of Henderson's outfit.'

The men were recovering from their shock. One reached for his holstered pistol. Coulter cocked his gun and the man halted his draw. The second man stepped quickly behind his companion for cover, and Coulter saw his right elbow bend as he pulled his gun. Clenching his teeth, Coulter triggered his Colt. His first slug hit the foremost man in the centre of the chest, and he fired again when he was able to draw a bead on the second man. Gun fire rocked the room as both men went down in a tangle of limbs. Coulter grabbed Julie by the arm and pulled her toward the door.

'Come on. We've got to get outa here,' he rapped.

Julie was sobbing with relief as Coulter turned and jerked open the door. The clerk was standing just outside the room, transfixed by the shooting that had occurred within. He was small, bald-headed, and his eyes were wide in shock. He backed away swiftly when Coulter appeared before him, raising his hands and shaking his head as he did so.

The echoes of the shots were still fading as Coulter, holding Julie's arm, ran from the lobby and pulled the girl out of the hotel. He turned left, and in a few seconds they were running through the darkness. He ducked into the nearest alley and they blundered along its length to the back lots. Coulter was breathing heavily when he halted, and Julie cannoned into him, grasped him with both hands, and dropped her head to his shoulder.

'They shot Doc down like a dog!' she gasped. 'It was cold-blooded murder.'

'How did they know you were in Doc's house?'

'They came in by the back door, wanting to know about our horses standing outside. They were looking around the town, they said, and saw our HM brand on my horse. Henderson's men have been searching for me ever since I plugged Jethro.'

Coulter was listening for approaching footsteps but heard nothing.

'This town is pulling at the reins,' he observed. 'Everyone is on his toes, expecting trouble, and we walked slap into the middle of it. We're gonna have to show some patience, Julie, or we

147

won't live to see the end of this. Let's get out of here and come back when the situation has cooled. Another week or so and we can pick our time and place.'

'I think you're right.' Julie's voice trembled as she spoke. Her breathing had eased and she stepped back from him. 'I dread to think what would have happened if you hadn't spotted them taking me into the hotel.'

'Don't worry about it,' he urged. 'Let's get out of here. No one else knows about our horses being at the doc's. Let's get them and hit the trail.'

'We need some provisions pretty badly, and the store will be closed now.' The practicalities of their situation lay uppermost in Julie's mind.

'What's to stop us going to the back door and demanding what we want?' he countered.

'Henderson's men will be out in force now. I think we'll be lucky to get away as it is. Doc was saying, when those two men burst in, that the Henderson outfit was thick around

148

town, and watching everything pretty closely.'

'And they'll probably make a search of the whole town when they get organized.' Coulter gnawed at his bottom lip as he considered. He was looking back along the alley as he spoke, and saw several figures cross the street end, which was faintly illuminated by a lamp on the sidewalk. 'We'd better get under cover somewhere and lie low until they quit searching. Got any ideas? We need to move pretty fast.'

'Bill Swain runs the general store. He's always spoken out against Henderson. I'm sure he'd help us out. There are a lot of folk against Henderson, but they are helpless to do anything on their own.'

'OK, so lead the way to the store. If Swain ain't keen to help, I can persuade him to give us some supplies.'

'We must be careful not to spread the trouble.' Julie sounded uneasy. 'If we put the honest folk against us we'll have no chance of coming out on top.'

'I'll take it easy.' Coulter followed closely as she started through the darkness of the back lots, staying close to the rear of the buildings fronting the main street. Dense shadows surrounded them like a cloak, and Coulter held Julie's arm in order to stay with her. She tripped and almost fell over some unseen obstruction, and Coulter saved her from a fall. Then he accidentally kicked a pile of empty cans, and they froze at the ensuing clatter. A dog started barking furiously close by, and Coulter clenched his teeth.

Julie started forward again and they moved slowly through the night.

Lamplight was showing from a rear window in the store when they finally reached it. Julie knocked at the back door. Coulter stood with his right hand on the butt of his pistol, convinced that they would find no help in this town. Several tense moments passed before there was a reaction from inside the store, and then they heard the sound of a bolt being withdrawn. The door was

150

opened just a crack and a bearded face peered warily out at them.

'It's Julie Wade, Bill.' Anxiety sounded in the girl's voice. 'I need help.'

The door was opened wide and the storekeeper reached out, grasped Julie's arm, and dragged her in through the doorway. He froze when he saw Coulter.

'Who's that with you, Julie?' he demanded.

'Jack Smith. He was working for us when Grandfather was killed, and he shot it out with Henderson's gunslingers. You can trust him.'

'Come in quick. There'll be hell to pay if you're seen. I've just looked out along the street and Henderson's men are running around like bees round a molasses jar. What is going on? The sheriff said last week that he arrested you because you shot Henderson, and then you were busted out of jail. I've never seen so many gunnies on the street before. It's getting so it ain't safe for anyone to be out on the sidewalks.'

'Two of Henderson's men just

murdered Doc Tracey.' Julie explained what had occurred.

Swain stifled a curse. Fear showed briefly in his dark eyes. He was tall and thin like a beanpole, with narrow, sloping shoulders and small hands.

'So we know what will happen to me if you're found in here,' he observed grimly.

Julie's face was chalky white and shock showed in her eyes. 'Give us some supplies, Bill, and we'll make ourselves scarce. I wouldn't want to put you and your family in danger, but we are desperate.'

'Sure. Come with me.' Swain led the way into the store. He picked up a gunny sack and began filling it with the items Julie required.

Coulter stood uneasily in the background, his hand close to the butt of his gun. He heard heavy footsteps outside on the sidewalk. Swain paused, set down the gunny sack, and placed a finger to his lips. A heavy hand tried the front door, and voices sounded when it was discovered that the door was locked. Knuckles rapped against the door.

'Come on, Swain. Open up. It's Thad Henderson. I ain't got all night. I know you're in there; I can see the light. We're checking the town for a killer. Two of our men have just been murdered in the hotel.'

Swain's face had turned deathly pale. He motioned for Julie and Coulter to return to the back room, his hands signalling caution. The knuckles rapped on the door again, sounding louder and more insistent. Swain picked up a double-barrelled Greener 12-gauge shotgun from behind the counter and checked its loads.

'Do you want me to bust down the door?' the voice continued. 'Open up!'

'Who in hell do you think you are, Henderson?' Swain demanded. 'Try busting down my door and you'll get a load of buckshot. I'm closed. Come back tomorrow.'

Coulter was moving toward the back door.

'We'd better leave while we can,' he said in an undertone to Julie. 'We can come back for supplies when Henderson has finished searching.'

'I'll have everything ready for you later,' Swain promised. 'Get out of town fast and stay away till just before sunup. I shall be up and about then and it'll be safer for you to move around.'

'Thanks, Bill. We'll do as you say.' Julie pressed close to Coulter as Swain opened the back door and peered around outside.

'Good luck,' he said as they departed.

Coulter led the way into dense shadow, and they were barely ten yards from the store when footsteps and voices sounded in the alley beside it. Two men appeared from the shadows and approached the back door of the store. Julie stifled a gasp. Coulter halted, and they stood motionless.

'What the hell is Swain playing at?' one of the men demanded. 'This job is bad enough without him making it worse.'

'He's on the town council, and they're all against Henderson,' the other replied. 'We won't find any help here, but we got to check him out.'

Coulter led Julie away as one of the men began hammering on the back door of the store. He did not like leaving Swain to face the wrath of Henderson's men but was aware that to resist now would start a war in the town. As they moved away they heard the sound of heavy blows. Henderson's men were carrying out their threat to break down Swain's door. Coulter halted abruptly, pulling Julie to a halt. It went against the grain to run out.

'I can't leave Swain to face that trouble on his own,' he said tersely. 'I've got to go back and help him. You make your way round to the back of the doctor's house and pick up your horse. Get out of town and ride to Morgan's place. Stay out of sight there until I show up.'

'What are you gonna do?' Julie sounded scared, and grasped his arm.

'I'm sure they won't harm Swain.'

The double blast of a shotgun shattered the silence and heavy echoes fled across the town.

'Get moving,' Coulter rapped. 'I'm going back.'

He turned abruptly and started running back towards the rear of the store, pistol in his hand. Lamp light was streaming out of the doorway of the building, and Coulter saw two men dragging Bill Swain outside. The storekeeper was struggling violently, and one of the men punched him on the jaw.

'Hold it,' Coulter called, and the sound of his voice halted them. 'Let him go.' Swain fell to the ground when he was released. Both men were trying to get a look at Coulter. The one on the right reached for his holstered pistol.

'Don't try it,' Coulter warned. 'I've got you covered.'

The man did not stay his movement. His pistol cleared leather and, as it began to level, Coulter fired a single shot. The gunslinger took the bullet in his chest and pitched to the ground. The second man raised his hands. Swain scrambled to his feet and dashed back into the store, to re-emerge a moment later holding his shotgun.

'Thanks, mister,' he said to Coulter. 'Thanks for your help. These men busted into my store. They were going to rob me. I can handle it now. I'll take this galoot along to the sheriff's office. I don't know what this town is coming to. It's getting so a man ain't safe in his own home.'

He jabbed the twin muzzles of the shotgun against the gunslinger's spine.

'Get moving,' he rapped. 'You know where the jail is. Start walking or I'll fill you full of buckshot.'

'I'm not a robber,' the man protested. 'I work for JH. We're looking for a killer who shot two of our men in the hotel.'

'Henderson's outfit ain't got the right to bust down doors and knock folk about,' Swain said calmly. 'You can tell your story to the sheriff.'

Coulter grinned and turned away. He hurried to the nearest alley and traversed it to the street, wanting to catch Julie before she rode out. He crossed the street and entered an alley opposite making his way to the rear of the doctor's house. Julie was in the act of mounting her horse and he called to her, his voice hoarse with tension. She turned swiftly and came running to him.

'Are you all right?' she demanded, clutching at him. 'I heard a pistol shot after you left me and figured you were dead.'

He explained what had occurred, and she sighed heavily and turned to walk back to her horse. Coulter followed her closely and caught up his reins. He would feel a lot easier when they were clear of town. Julie mounted and, as he put his left foot in the stirrup, the shadows around him seemed to erupt with movement. Three men rushed him. One grasped his bridle. Coulter, caught off-balance, reached for his pistol. The other men grappled with him. One gripped his arms, pinioning them to his side. The other swung a drawn gun and slammed it heavily against Coulter's head. A thousand stars exploded inside his skull, flaring like a Fourth of July firework display. Pain erupted inside his skull, but vanished almost immediately as he plunged head-first into a black pit that yawned suddenly at his feet. Sight and sound faded as he slumped into unconsciousness . . .

Throbbing pain in his head dragged Coulter back to his senses. He could hear the harsh sound of men's voices nagging and chafing the silence, and forced open his eyes to take in his surroundings. He was lying on the floor of the law office. Men were standing around him, some holding pistols. He recognised the massive figure of Sheriff Coombe, whose fleshy face carried a brooding expression. Another face floated above him and he clenched his teeth. It was Luke Doyle.

'Get him on his feet,' Doyle rasped. 'He's coming round. He's Wayne Coulter right enough.'

'The last of Blackjack Dawson's gang,' Coombe observed. 'He's the one busted Julie Wade outa here last week, and put a slug in my shoulder. Henderson put a price of five hundred dollars on his head. We'll share that between us, Doyle. Stick him in a cell and slam the door on him, and then bring Julie Wade in here. I wanta ask her a lot of questions.'

'I heard Henderson say he'd pay three hundred dollars for a sight of her,' Doyle responded. 'It looks like clean-up time around here.'

Coulter was dragged to his feet. His senses swirled as he came upright. A pistol was stuck in his back and he was pushed across the office to the cells. Rough hands grasped him and he was manhandled into a cell and thrown roughly on a bunk. The cell door clanged shut and he heard the metallic sound of a key being turned in the lock.

He lay motionless until his head stopped spinning, and then eased himself into a sitting position.

Lamplight filled the cells with a harsh yellow glare that hurt his eyes, and Coulter shielded them with his hands as he looked around. Bill Swain was standing disconsolately in the next cell, gripping the bars as he watched Coulter, and his face carried desperation in its expression.

'What happened to you?' Coulter demanded.

'Coombe didn't believe me. He stuck me in here to cool off. I was hoping you'd get clear.'

Coulter leaned back on the bunk and closed his eyes. His half-healed shoulder wound was throbbing ominously from the rough treatment he had received.

'Did they bring Julie in here?' he demanded.

'Yeah.' Swain sighed heavily. 'They took her into the office when they brought you in here. Coombe is bullying her, but I don't think she'll break. I won't be in here too long, and when I get out I'll take legal steps to put this situation right.'

'You better keep that under your hat or you won't make it to the front door,' Coulter warned. 'It looks like Henderson is playing for keeps and doesn't care who knows it.'

Swain subsided and sat down on the bunk in his cell. Coulter massaged his skull. His probing fingers found a blood-matted area behind his right ear. His head ached intolerably and he closed his eyes. When the connecting door between the cells and the office crashed open he looked up to see Doyle and Al Billing coming to the door of his cell. Doyle was grinning, swaggering as he gripped the bars. Billing stood in the background looking uneasy, his eyes narrowed and watchful.

'You've been playing the wrong kind of game, Coulter,' Doyle said. 'You shot the sheriff, busted a gal out of here, and set yourself up against Jethro

Henderson, the biggest operator in the county. You was sure asking for trouble, and now you got a big load of it on your plate. Why didn't you get the hell out when you got away from the rail depot?'

'One thing kept me here,' Coulter gritted. 'You sold out the gang, Doyle, and I won't pull stakes until you're on Boot Hill, where you belong. I owe it to Blackjack to put you in your grave. I knew you were wrong the minute you joined the gang, but Blackjack wouldn't listen to me, and he's paid the price for that, but your turn is coming.'

Doyle laughed, but it sounded false and he looked uneasy.

'You ain't going any place but to the spot you just mentioned,' he retorted. 'Boot Hill, you said. Well, I reckon you'll be there long before I get round to trading my gun for a harp. You've got a pile of murders lined up at your door, and they won't waste any time hitting you with the charges.'

'What are you doing with Julie

Wade?' Coulter demanded.

'Worried about her, are you?' Doyle grinned as he rubbed his big hands together. 'And so you should be. She shot Jethro Henderson and he wants her blood. I doubt if she'll see another sun-up. We're waiting for Thad Henderson to come and pick her up. He'll probably want you, too, the way you shot the hell out of his outfit. I told the sheriff from the start that it was you behind the killings. Now we've got you for it, and the law will put you out of my way.'

Doyle turned and swaggered out of the cell block. Billing remained for a moment, looking as if he had something on his mind. He said nothing, but winked at Coulter before departing. Coulter sighed heavily and sat down on his bunk when the connecting door was slammed. He could hear raised voices coming from the law office, and strained his ears for the sound of Julie's voice, but all he heard was the booming tone of Sheriff Coombe's harsh voice.

Coulter tried to relax but was too worried about Julie, and when silence finally settled in the front office he stood up and grasped the bars of the cell door. Frustration hit him hard and he shook the door impotently, and then began pacing the small cell like a caged puma separated from her cubs. The silence grated against his nerves. He felt as if he were sitting on a keg of gunpowder with a lighted fuse under him, but finally controlled his feelings and sat down again, although restlessness still gripped him, filling him with real fear for Julie's safety. Wild impulses darted through him, and he felt that any chance to escape would be worth the risk that might be involved.

Time passed unmeasured, and Coulter dozed despite his worries. When the sound of the connecting door being opened aroused him, he arose from the bunk and went to the door of the cell. Al Billing appeared and came hurrying to him.

'I ain't got much time,' Billing said.

'Doyle and Coombe have taken Julie to Jethro Henderson at the hotel. How much is it worth to you to get out of here right now, Wayne? Promise to pay me when you get to Newton and I'll spring you.'

'You name a price,' Coulter responded. 'How much do you want?'

'I can't stick around here after you're gone, which means I'll miss out on some mighty rich pickings, so I figure a thousand bucks should fix it. Whaddya say?'

'The money is yours.' Coulter spoke without hesitation. 'Get me out of here, Al, and the money is as good as in your pocket.'

Billing grinned. 'Doyle don't really trust me,' he said. 'I ain't a fool, and some of the things Doyle has been saying make me think he'll give me the chop when it suits him. So I'm looking out for myself. They've left me in charge here while they're away and Doyle took the cell keys with him, but I got the spare bunch, and you're on your way out this minute.'

Billing unlocked the cell door. Coulter stepped forward to leave, but paused and studied Billing's intent face.

'What's wrong, Wayne?' Billing demanded.

'A thought just struck me, Al. Are you playing this straight?'

'What the hell do you mean? Do you think I'm another Luke Doyle? Heck, I'm laying my life on the line to get a measly thousand bucks from you. If I'm caught springing you I'll get it in the neck. These guys around here are playing a real tough game. Now how about it? Do you wanta get out before Coombe and Doyle come back? I'm gonna have to pull out as well, and I need a good head start.'

'OK. I'll trust you.' Coulter left the cell and hurried into the front office. He saw his gunbelt and pistol looped over a hook in the wall behind the desk and went for it.

Billing crossed to the street door and eased it open a crack to peer out.

'Make it quick, Wayne,' he urged. 'Them buzzards will be coming back any minute. Hit the street and keep going. I guess you got your horse stashed somewhere close. I'll be waiting for you in Newton.'

'I'll be there,' Coulter replied.

He hurried across to the door and slipped outside into the shadows on the sidewalk. Billing slammed the door and a heavy bolt was rammed home. Coulter paused, for Billing should have been at his heels, also making a run for it. Before he could react, Julie's voice screamed out from nearby shadows.

'Jack, it's a trap. They've set you up.'

Coulter ducked and drew his gun as a reddish ribbon of muzzle flame split the darkness to his right. A slug smacked into the office door beside him. He dropped to one knee to return fire, but his hammer fell upon an empty cylinder and he cursed Billing for his treachery. He had been set up with an empty gun . . .

8

Coulter dropped flat as he grabbed fresh shells from his cartridge belt. The darkness on both sides of his position was tattered by flashing guns, and bullets struck the front of the office as raucous echoes fled through the night. He cursed Al Billing as he loaded the pistol, and then rolled across the sidewalk and fell into the dust of the street, jarring his half-healed shoulder. He levelled the gun and began to return fire. Hammering shots blasted out the silence, and muzzle flame speared through the night like red stabs of pure hell.

Sweat beaded Coulter's forehead as he aimed and fired at pistol flashes, but he was aware that he had to get moving, and fast. There were so many Henderson gunnies in town he would not be able to move without falling over some of them. But he was pinned down from both sides, and winced when a slug burned his left forearm. Another plunked through the tall crown of his hat and he ducked.

He rolled into the gap beneath the sidewalk, although there was little space to move, and squirmed like a snake to get moving from the danger area. Guns still fired at the spot where he had been lying, and he realized that if he had not moved he would certainly be dead. Slugs were hammering into the surrounding woodwork like lethal rain.

His thoughts were remote as he crawled to his left. Billing had sold him out. So now he had another reason for sticking around. He was halted when the space under the sidewalk grew even smaller, and had to force himself along, the boards jamming against his back and sending pain through his left shoulder. He twisted to his left and pushed for the back of the sidewalk, and suddenly his head was in the open and he found himself peering into the darkness of the alley beside the jail. He was dimly aware that the shooting had ceased, although his ears were still protesting.

He got to his feet and went along the alley to the back lots, moving slowly and feeling his way with his left hand. Men were calling out on the street, and he recognised Coombe's heavy tone. He began to run, throwing caution away as the desire to get clear filled him. He had to do something fast about getting Julie away from her captors.

The back lots swallowed him up and he paused to reload his pistol, thankful that Billing had not emptied the loops on his cartridge belt as well as removing the loads from his six-gun. He moved more slowly along the rear of the buildings fronting the street until he reached the back of the hotel. Lights were showing in several windows overlooking the rear, and he wondered where Jethro Henderson's room was situated, aware that it was time Henderson was put out of it. With the big boss dead the organization should fall apart.

Gun in hand, Coulter moved to the back door and tried it. The door opened easily and he stepped inside the building, his breathing restrained and his reflexes honed to the highest peak of alertness. This was where it began, and he would make no mistakes as he stalked the man who was responsible for all the trouble that had hit him and Julie . . .

A flight of stairs led up from the corridor to the top floor, and he ascended them two at a time, sacrificing silence for speed, aware that he did not have much time. He expected Julie to be in Henderson's room now, and if he acted quickly he could kill Henderson and get the girl away before anyone could stop him. But first he had to find Henderson's room.

A corridor at the top of the stairs led left and right and Coulter paused and peered around. Two men were off to the right, lounging on chairs outside a door on the left side of the corridor that gave access to the room overlooking the street. Henderson's room, he guessed and, at that moment the door was opened and two men emerged from the room. Coulter grinned tensely, for one of the men was holding Julie's arm and using considerable strength to move her along. The girl was struggling like a wildcat and cursing Henderson and his outfit.

Coulter remained out of view and watched as Julie was removed to a room opposite. He could not approach the room while the two guards were outside Henderson's door so he eased back and descended the stairs to leave the building. He made for the street by way of an alley, crossed it, and looked up at the front of the hotel.

Lighted windows marked the rooms overlooking the street. Coulter deduced that the window to his right was in the room Henderson occupied, and one of those on his left was where Julie was being held. There was a balcony in front of the rooms, and Coulter moved back across the street to make an approach.

A flight of wooden steps on the left led up to the balcony and Coulter ascended. He paused beside the nearest window on his left and looked into the room to see Julie, now bound hand and foot, lying on a bed. Her two captors were seated at a table, playing cards. Coulter moved to his right and looked into the room he suspected was where Jethro Henderson had installed himself, and saw the big rancher lying propped up in a bed with a swath of bandaging around his upper chest. Two gunnies were present in the room, and Coulter recognized them as Thad Henderson and Jessop, the gunnie who had killed a townsman in the crowd earlier.

Coulter was aware that it would have been a simple matter to gun down all three men in the room and escape before anyone could recover from the shock, but Julie's presence in the hotel complicated matters, and he was keenly aware that he needed to get her to

174

safety before taking action. He crossed to the room where Julie was being held and tried the handle of the door that gave access to the balcony. The door opened, and one of the two men at the table looked up quickly.

Coulter drew his gun and stepped into the room. Both men started to their feet but the sight of Coulter's gun made them change their minds about resisting and they both dropped back on their chairs and raised their hands.

'One at a time, get rid of your guns,' Coulter ordered.

The men obeyed without hesitation. Coulter motioned with his pistol.

'Free the girl,' he rasped.

One of the men almost overturned his chair in his eagerness to obey. Julie came to Coulter's side, smiling now, and picked up the pistols her captors had dropped.

'Tie them tight while I watch them.' Coulter took the guns from her and stuck them in his belt as she obeyed him.

When they were ready to leave, Coulter warned the men to remain silent and led Julie out to the balcony. They descended to the street and paused in the shadows.

'I want you to get out of town as fast as you can,' Coulter told her. 'I can't operate with you loose and likely to find more trouble. I could have killed Jethro Henderson a few moments ago, but I needed to free you so I had to change my mind or he would be dead now.'

'You should have shot him,' she said callously. 'I was handed over to Thad Henderson and that pet killer of his, Jessop, and they took me into the hotel to face Jethro, who told them to take me out on the range, kill me, and bury me deep. Give me a gun and I'll go up to Jethro's room now and finish him off.'

'Like I said, I can do the job more easily if you're not around.' Coulter spoke as if she had not protested. 'I won't leave any loose ends. I'll handle those top gunmen, and when the smoke clears there'll be no Hendersons left to cause more trouble. Then I'll clean up on Doyle and Billing, and after that we can shake the dust of this town off our boots. I'll go with you to the doc's house to check if the horses are still there, and when you're hauling your freight I'll make a start on the clean-up.'

Julie did not protest as they hurried through the shadows. They crossed the street, entered an alley and traversed it to the back lots, and then moved slowly through the shadows to the rear of the doctor's house. Drawing close, Coulter put a hand on Julie's arm and halted her by a rear corner of the house.

'Someone is over by the horses,' he whispered in her ear.

'How do you know?' she asked. 'I didn't hear a thing.'

'My bay warned me. He snuffled, and I know every sound he makes and what they mean. Stay put here and I'll sneak in close and check it out.'

'Don't leave me without a gun,' she pleaded.

After a moment's consideration, Coulter drew one of the pistols from his belt and gave it to her.

'Don't shoot me by mistake when I come back,' he said in an undertone, and moved away into the darkness.

Although his eyes were accustomed to the shadows, Coulter found it difficult to pierce the gloom for details of his surroundings. He heard the thump of a hoof just ahead, and suddenly realized that his pistol was in his hand although he had no recollection of drawing it. He breathed shallowly through his mouth and his ears were strained for the slightest unnatural sound. He expected an ambusher to be watching the horses but not close in, and began to make a circle around the waiting animals.

He reached the side of a small building, and a gun muzzle came out of the shadows and was jabbed painfully against his left side.

'Hold it,' a voice warned. 'Who in hell are you sneaking around here in the dark?'

'Thad Henderson sent me to watch these horses,' Coulter replied in a hoarse whisper. 'There's a killer loose in town. Who are you?'

'Al Billing. Coulter is the killer, and I need to get him before he gets me.'

Coulter clenched his teeth, wondering what kindly fate had delivered one of his enemies into his hands. The gun muzzle was removed from his side. He could see Billing's outline faintly, and reached out to snatch the man's gun from his hand, simultaneously thrusting forward his pistol to cover him.

'Tough luck, Al,' Coulter said. 'You're in a tight fix right now.'

'Coulter? Jeez! Where did you come from? I figured you'd be long gone by now.'

'I ain't leaving unfinished business behind. First you, and then Doyle. After that I'll begin to make plans, but right now I can't see any further than you two old pards.'

'Now listen, Wayne, I had to set you up. Doyle wanted me to prove I was on

179

the level with him so I had to drop you in it. I knew they couldn't kill you. You're too good for the likes of them. I thought you'd nail Doyle and then split the breeze out of town. I turned you loose, didn't I?'

'Yeah, with an unloaded pistol. What kind of a chance was that? Doyle must have offered you a big wad of dough to go against me.'

'Heck, there was nothing personal in it. I'm flat broke, and I got to go where the dough is. I didn't like turning on you, but I've got to line my pockets so I can pull out. Gimme five hundred bucks now and I'll go shoot Doyle for you, and throw in the sheriff for free.'

'I can take care of my own dirty work. I don't trust you now, Al. I've got to put you out of it.'

'You wouldn't shoot a pard in cold blood, would you? We rode together a long time, Wayne. We pulled a lotta jobs together. Listen, it ain't just the law you got to fight in this set-up. Jethro Henderson has taken over the town, and he's planning on wiping out everyone who's against him. That means a lot of honest folks are gonna die, including that gal of yours. Henderson's men took her to the hotel just before I turned you loose at the jail. I reckon, by now, she's on her way to an early grave out on the range.'

'Try telling me something I don't know.' Coulter lifted his gun hand in a swift movement and slammed the barrel of his pistol against Billing's head. Billing cried out; his knees gave way and he fell against Coulter, who struck again. Billing groaned and fell heavily to the ground. Coulter bent over him and checked him out. Billing was unconscious.

Coulter straightened, and then paused, for a straying beam of light glinted on the deputy badge Billing was wearing. A thought struck him and he grinned. Removing the badge from Billing's shirt front, he pinned it to his vest, thinking it might give him an edge in a tight spot if he came up against any of Henderson's men.

He completed the circle around the horses and was satisfied that Billing had come alone to the spot. He made his way back to where he had left Julie and, as he neared the corner of the house, the girl called out tensely.

'Hold it right there. I got a gun on you.'

Coulter halted. 'Hey, it's me — Jack,' he replied in an undertone. 'Don't go skittish on me.'

'I can see a law badge on you,' she replied.

'I just picked it up.' He grinned. 'It might come in useful later.'

Julie emerged from the shadows with a levelled gun, and Coulter escorted her to the horses.

'I don't want to go,' she protested. 'Two guns are better than one, and the least I can do is cover your back. Let me stay with you, Jack. If I don't kill Henderson I shall regret it for the rest of my life. You've got your own chores to do, so leave me mine.'

'I want to go around town knowing

that everyone I come up against is an enemy,' he responded. 'Don't make this any harder than it has to be. Ride out now and I'll meet up with you later. Stop off where we hid out earlier just clear of town. Get in your saddle now and move out.'

Protesting, Julie swung into her saddle and took up her reins. Her face was a pale blur in the shadows as she looked down at Coulter.

'Don't get killed,' she said softly. 'Good luck.'

She urged the horse into motion and Coulter watched until she vanished into the night. When the soft thud of hoofs had faded he heaved a long sigh and returned his attention to the job in hand. He drew his pistol and went back to where Billing was lying. The outlaw was beginning to stir, and Coulter pressed his muzzle against the man's forehead. Sweat beaded his brow as he tried to squeeze his trigger, but realized that he could not kill Billing in cold blood. He eased his hammer forward and waited for Billing to regain his senses.

'Get on your feet, Al,' he said at length. 'I won't shoot you if you promise to get out of town right now and keep riding.'

'Sure, Wayne, anything you say. You won't see or hear me after this. I can see the way the wind is blowing, and it ain't good. I'm on my way.'

Billing turned and faded into the shadows. Coulter stood listening, aware that he might well be making a mistake. When full silence returned he led his bay along an alley to the street and tethered it with other horses in front of the saloon in case he needed to make a fast getaway.

He was checking the brands on the other horses — all carried JH — when three men emerged from the saloon, and Coulter stood with his back to them until they had passed along the sidewalk. They were heading towards the law office, and he heard one of them make a remark.

'What for we gotta string up Swain? He's only a storekeeper.'

'He's on the town council,' one of the others replied, 'and we've got to get rid of anybody who can stand up against JH. You heard what Jessop said, so let's get on with it. The sheriff has come out on our side and he's afraid of a kick-back from the few honest men around. We've got to clear the ground for a complete take-over, and that means dealing with anyone who's against us.'

Coulter was shocked by what he overheard, and followed the men along the sidewalk. He stepped into the alley beside the law office when the trio entered the building, and eased forward to peer through the window into the office to observe the proceedings. Coombe was seated at his desk and Doyle was standing beside it. Coulter could not hear what was being said but Coombe listened to the trio, and then waved a hand in the direction of the cell block.

Doyle picked up a bunch of keys off a corner of the desk and let himself into the cells, to emerge moments later ushering a complaining Bill Swain into the office. Two of the three JH men grasped Swain and led him to the door. The third man spoke again to the sheriff, and Coombe got to his feet, opened a cupboard in the rear wall of the office and produced a lariat, which he handed over.

Coulter watched the two gunnies drag Swain out to the sidewalk. The storekeeper struggled vainly, and one of the men struck him a solid blow that stunned him. They dragged him along the sidewalk, followed by the man with the rope, and Coulter tagged along behind.

The trio paused when they reached the front of the bank, and the man with the rope tossed it up over an overhanging ledge of the balcony. Coulter moved in closer, his gun in hand. Swain was stunned. His knees would not take his weight, and the two

186

men held him upright while the rope was put around his neck. Coulter hurried forward, and the three gunnies swung round at the sound of his boots on the sidewalk.

'Get the hell outa here, mister,' one of them warned, and then caught a gleam of the law badge on Coulter's chest. 'Say, you're just in time to make this legal,' he added. 'The sheriff told us to bring Swain out here and hang him as an example to the rest of the town. Come and put your weight on the rope when we swing Swain up.'

'Drop the rope,' Coulter ordered. 'Get your hands up. You ain't hanging anybody. Swain is an honest man.'

One of the two men holding Swain upright jerked his elbow and reached for his holstered gun. Coulter saw the other two men reaching for weapons and triggered his pistol without hesitation. Gun flashes tore through the gloom and the raucous crash of shots blasted out the heavy silence. Coulter narrowed his eyes and swung his pistol.

The man putting the rope around Swain's neck suddenly lost interest in the proceedings, twisted, and slanted down into the dust of the street, his gun falling from his hand.

Swain recovered his senses at that moment and broke free from the men holding him. He flailed his arms, knocking one man's gun out of his grasp. Coulter squeezed his trigger and a .45 slug thudded into the man's chest. The second man turned his gun on Swain but the storekeeper blocked the move, and Coulter shot the gunnie before he could overpower Swain.

The echoes of the shooting faded slowly. Coulter restrained his breathing, for his nostrils were filled with the stench of burned powder. He went to Swain and took the rope from around the man's neck.

'They were gonna string me up,' Swain gasped unsteadily. 'Me — an honest man! What's going on around here? Has everyone gone loco? Coombe let me out of the jail for these men to

188

hang me! Earlier, I saw Jessop gun down an innocent man in cold blood just for talking against Henderson.'

'That's how I saw it,' Coulter said. 'So you'd better round up all the honest men you can find and organize them to fight Henderson and the sheriff. I'll go back to the law office and take care of Coombe and Doyle. Henderson won't have so much force backing him if the law department is cleaned up. Get someone who is honest to take over the sheriff's job until you can sort out this bad business. And you better get moving. Time is running out.'

Swain nodded and started along the sidewalk. Coulter went after him and pulled him up.

'Not along the street,' Coulter warned. 'You'll be a target for every gun backing Henderson.'

Swain turned and hurried into an alley. Coulter stood listening to the man's boots thudding away into the shadows until silence returned. He holstered his gun and started along the sidewalk.

A figure was standing in the doorway of the law office, watching Coulter's approach. Coulter recognized Doyle, who was probably checking on the shooting from the safety of the law office. Coulter drew his pistol and cocked it, aware that he could shoot Doyle without compunction, but wanted the man to know who was going to kill him.

'Hey, Doyle, it's time to trade lead,' Coulter called. 'You've come to the end of your rope. You owe me for that gun trap you set up at the rail depot and I'm here to collect. Come out of that doorway and pull your gun. You'll get an even break, which is more than you deserve.'

Doyle jumped back out of the doorway and the next instant he was shooting at Coulter from cover. Coulter had expected such a move, and dropped to one knee. He bracketed the doorway with three quick shots. Doyle stepped into view with a jerky movement, as if he had lost control of his legs. He swung to face Coulter, trying to lift his pistol into the aim.

Coulter triggered his Colt in a sudden frenzy, emptying the cylinder in a cold rage, and three .45 slugs tore into Doyle's left arm and chest. Coulter's hammer struck an empty cartridge and he began to reload instinctively, his narrowed gaze on Doyle as the outlaw went down on the sidewalk.

There was a picture of Blackjack Dawson in the forefront of Coulter's mind as he pushed himself upright and continued to the law office. As far as he was concerned his work here in town was over, but there was still a lot of dirty business to be settled. He had been shot at by Henderson's bunch, and they were here, just waiting to be confronted.

He went forward intent on killing the sheriff, and then gun play exploded in the shadows just ahead, and two guns began tossing lead at him. He went down and rolled in the dust, and then came up on his elbows and began shooting at flashes. This was where it all started, and he would not quit until the last gunnie was dead.

9

Coulter paused after the first quick volley of shots and got up to dive for the cover of an alley. Slugs crackled around him but he kept moving, and peered along the street towards the jail. He saw Doyle stretched out inertly and grinned. Nothing else mattered if Doyle was dead. He could now go on about Julie's business, and when Jethro Henderson was dead the girl would be set free from her desire for revenge.

He traversed the alley to the back lot and flattened himself against a rear wall in deeper shadow. The shooting was over for now, but still rang in his head. He walked through the darkness to the rear of the hotel, tried the back door to the building and found it locked. He turned into an alley and headed for the street. Reaching the alley mouth at the street end, he paused, and at that precise moment a man slid around the corner off the sidewalk and cannoned into him.

Coulter's pistol leapt into his hand and he jabbed the muzzle against the man's stomach.

'Who are you and what are you doing sneaking around?' Coulter demanded.

'I work for Jethro Henderson,' the man replied. 'There's a killer loose on the street somewhere, and he's shooting up the JH outfit. You're a deputy, ain't you?'

'I'm wearing a law badge,' Coulter admitted. 'What are you doing?'

'I'm fetching a buckboard to take Jethro Henderson outa town. Thad Henderson is running things while Jethro is out of the saddle, and he's got a meaner streak down his back than his old man. The fur is gonna fly around here when Jethro is back safe on the ranch.'

Coulter holstered his gun and the man went on his way. So Jethro Henderson was running scared from the town. Coulter grinned as he went into the street. If he added to the rancher's disquiet, maybe the whole outfit would pull out. He crossed the street, keeping to the denser shadows, and worked his way along alley-mouth by alley-mouth until he was facing the hotel.

There was a guard on the balcony. Coulter could see his silhouette against a lighted window. He drew his pistol and fired two shots through the window of Jethro's room, and turned his weapon on the guard when the man began shooting in reply. The guard fell off the balcony and thudded in the street. The lamp in Jethro's room was extinguished. A gun opened up on Coulter's position from the right at street level, and he faded back into the alley and moved out fast. He had just cleared the alley at the rear end when someone at the street end emptied a six-gun along its length, and slugs crackled and whined through the night.

Coulter moved to the right and

traversed the next alley along to get back to the street. He paused in its mouth and looked across at the hotel, which was now to his left. Four men were standing in front of the hotel, all holding guns, and one of them was Thad Henderson, recognizable by the twin guns around his waist. Reloading his spent chambers, Coulter turned his gun loose on the figures. Gun flashes and booming reports cut through the night, and two of men went down on the sidewalk.

The remaining pair dived for cover through the hotel doorway, but Thad Henderson was one of the two left lying on the sidewalk. Coulter eased back into cover as slugs came hammering around the alley mouth in reply. He ran swiftly along the alley to the back lots and moved to his left, passing the alley he had first used, and headed for the next one along to the left.

Gun echoes were still grumbling across the town when he reached the street again. A glance around revealed that the street was now deserted. Coulter reloaded his gun and waited patiently, but long minutes passed and he began to feel that he had to press home his attack. He had declared war on JH and needed to retain the initiative. He left the alley and walked openly along the sidewalk through dense shadows, passed the hotel, and headed for an alley opposite the law office.

Luke Doyle had been removed from the sidewalk in front of the office, and Coulter hoped the renegade was dead. The big window on the right in the office had been broken by the shots Al Billing fired earlier. Coulter drew his gun and emptied its loads into the front of the building, shooting holes in the door and smashing the remaining window. Echoes fled as he reloaded, and gun smoke was thick in his nostrils as he checked his surroundings.

He saw figures on the street down at the hotel, and two men started towards the law office. Coulter reckoned they could only be JH gunnies, and sent two shots in their direction. One man spun around and hit the dust. The other faded into an alley, and the next instant a stream of lead came thudding and crackling in Coulter's direction. He sought cover and waited.

Passing along an alley to the back lots, he again passed the hotel before regaining the street to check it from a different angle. No one was in sight on the street, and there was no movement anywhere. He was tempted to shoot some more holes in the hotel, at Henderson's room in particular, but wanted the rancher to be brought out, so held his fire. He sensed that he held the initiative.

Hoofbeats sounded along the street to his left, and Coulter frowned as he listened. Two riders were coming into town at a walk. He eased back into denser shadows and waited patiently, his gun ready in his hand. Presently, the riders materialized out of the gloom and Coulter narrowed his eyes to pick out details. When the pair passed a lantern burning on the opposite side of the street he bent slightly at the knees to get them in silhouette, and a chill spread through his chest when he saw one was a woman. He thought immediately of Julie, and cocked his gun.

The second rider looked like Al Billing, and sweat broke out on Coulter's brow when light shone fleetingly on the man's face — it was Billing, and Julie was with the outlaw.

Coulter went forward to the edge of the sidewalk, his pistol levelled.

'Hey, Al,' he called sharply. 'Over here. It's Coulter. Come on over. I've got a gun on you.'

Billing reined in and, for a moment, remained motionless. Then he said something in an undertone to Julie and they turned their horses and came across the street. Coulter looked around. The street was still deserted, but he suspected that hostile eyes were watching all movement.

'Howdy, Wayne,' Billing greeted as he

reined up in front of Coulter. He was careful to keep his hands away from his waist. 'I met this little lady outside of town and she told me all about you. She wanted to come back to find you, and I decided to help her. I've been thinking over the situation, and I reckon my best bet is to go along with you. I ain't got no chance with anyone else.'

'You ain't got a hope from any angle,' Coulter told him flatly. 'I don't trust you now, Al, so cut your losses and get to hell out of here before I start shooting. I'm busy right now, and you're in my way.'

'I heard the shooting from way back,' Billing chuckled. 'How's it going?'

'Doyle went down, but I don't know if he's dead — likewise Thad Henderson.'

'You need to finish Coombe and Jethro Henderson to make any impact on this bunch,' Billing commented.

'I'm working on it. Now get out of here, Al. You're all washed up as far as

I'm concerned.' Coulter let his gaze slide to the motionless Julie. 'Why have you come back?' he demanded. 'You were well out of it.'

'I heard the shooting. It sounded so bad from out of town, and I was worried about you.'

'It's a lot worse around the street, and it is gonna be real bad before it's over,' he responded. 'You should have stayed away, but I won't send you out again while Al is hanging around. He might just try to collect the dough Henderson has put on your head.'

'I wouldn't do that, Wayne,' Billing cut in. 'It's not my style.'

'I must know you better than you know yourself,' Coulter retorted. 'You'd do anything to get yourself a stake right now. Why are you still hanging around? I told you to get going, so move out before I look at you through gunsmoke.'

Billing held up a hand. 'OK, I know when I'm not wanted. Be seeing you, pard. Don't take any wooden nickels.'

Billing backed up his horse several

yards before turning and riding back the way he had come. When the sound of hoofs had faded to nothing, Coulter looked up at Julie, who was motionless on her horse.

'How did Billing meet you?' he demanded.

'I was waiting out of town and he came riding by. I called to him, thinking he was you, and he brought me back into town.'

'So what do we do with you now? I'm in the middle of fighting JH, and so far I've done pretty good. They're figuring on taking Jethro Henderson back to his spread in a wagon because it's got too dangerous for him around here.'

'Then it's a good thing I came back,' Julie countered. 'I'll be waiting when they bring him out of the hotel.'

'Don't let's go through that again. Where can you hole up until this is done? There must be somewhere in town where you'll be safe.'

She stepped down from her saddle and turned to face him.

'There's nowhere I can hide. I'll stick with you now and we'll finish off the Henderson outfit together.'

'Tie your horse to that hitch rail and let's get off the street,' Coulter said quietly. 'We need to be in cover from here on in. I've been putting pressure on them, but I reckon it's time to get serious. I turned Bill Swain loose from the jail; and he went off to try and get some honest townsmen to back him.'

'I don't think he'll have much luck.' Julie hitched her horse to a rail and loosened the saddle girth. She drew a Winchester from the saddle scabbard and tucked the butt under her right arm. 'How many of Henderson's outfit are in town?'

Coulter grinned. 'I haven't had time to count them,' he retorted. 'I need to check out the law office to find out if I killed Doyle. Him and the sheriff have got to go before there'll be any chance for Swain to have an effect on Henderson by legal means. Let's move along the back lots.'

He turned and entered the nearest alley and Julie followed him closely. By now, Coulter was accustomed to the alleys on either side of the street, and walked resolutely through the shadows. He turned into the alley that gave access to the street on the far side of the law office, and paused in the shadows at the street-end. Julie crowded him to take a look around.

'You've smashed the windows of the law office. Is anyone alive in there?'

'I'm not going across to ask.' Coulter checked the street, and thought he saw furtive movement in front of the hotel. 'They'll probably move Henderson out by the back door. They can hardly use the street while I've got it covered.'

'Shall I go and check the rear while you stay here?' Julie suggested, and Coulter grasped her arm as she began to move away.

'No. Stay here and keep watch. I'll check it out. Don't make a move, whatever you might see. Just watch, and keep quiet if anyone comes prowling around.'

'I can do that.' She nodded. 'Make some noise when you come back. Don't creep up on me, whatever you do.'

'OK. See you shortly.'

Coulter turned and faded into the shadows to the right. He walked twenty yards before crossing the street, and then made for the nearest alley, losing himself in its dense shadows. He paused for a final look around the street to satisfy himself that the JH bunch was not gathering, and then made for the back lots.

There were lights shining out from the rear windows of the hotel, but no sign of a wagon at the back door. Coulter went close, moving carefully, and checked out the area thoroughly. He tried the back door, found it locked, and backed off to the alley at the side. As he entered the alley a hand came out of the darkness and stuck the muzzle of a pistol in his stomach; at the same time his gun was grasped and twisted out of his hand.

'Who in hell are you, sneaking

around here?' a harsh voice demanded.

'I'm Al Billing, a deputy sheriff,' Coulter answered quickly, and a hand touched his shirt briefly to check out the badge he was wearing. 'I'm trying to get a line on whoever is doing all the shooting around the street.'

'That killer has been playing up hell, whoever he is,' the gunnie replied. 'Thad Henderson was shot through the chest, although he's still on his feet. We're taking Jethro back to the ranch soon as the buckboard shows up, and then Jessop is gonna make a big search of the town to weed out those who are against JH.'

'Sounds like a vehicle coming now,' Coulter said, catching the sound of wheels on hard ground. 'Give me my gun and I'll get on.'

Coulter's pistol was handed back to him and he holstered the weapon and went on along the alley to the street. He stepped on to the sidewalk in front of the hotel and paused to look around. A man was standing in the doorway of the hotel, gun in hand, and levelled his weapon immediately he saw Coulter, but turned away when he spotted the law badge on Coulter's shirt front.

Coulter decided not to push his luck further and turned away to cross the street. He entered the shadows on the opposite side and made his way back to where he had left Julie. When he reached the alley-mouth where she had been waiting he paused and looked around, calling her name softly. There was no reply.

'Julie, where are you?' he repeated.

The breeze blew coldly around him, sounding desolate in the heavy silence and carrying the acrid smell of the burnt-out stable in its breath. Coulter leaned his right shoulder against a wall while he looked around and considered. Had Julie gone off of her own volition or had she been taken by either the law or Henderson's hardcases? He did not think she could have been taken quietly, and he had not heard any unnatural sounds, so it seemed fairly obvious that she had decided to go hunting alone.

Coulter was aware that with Julie unaccounted for, his free-ranging attack on JH had come to an end because he dared not press anywhere for fear of hitting the girl accidentally. Before she rode back into town, he had known that everyone he came across was a potential enemy; but now he had to consider her before making any move.

He went along the street to the law office. A lamp was burning inside, producing a feeble yellow glow. Someone was pacing to and fro inside, for he could hear the sound of boots treading on broken glass. Coulter eased forward to take a look into the office, and saw Doyle, heavily bandaged, with one arm in a sling, standing over Julie, who was seated on a chair before the desk. Sheriff Coombe was sitting behind the desk. Doyle was handling Julie roughly, shaking her by a shoulder with his good arm and threatening her.

'We know Coulter is working with you,' Doyle was saying. 'He's been shooting the JH outfit, and it's him out there now, causing all the trouble in town. He's like a wolf among sheep. So you better come clean, if you know what's good for you. Where is Coulter right now? Start talking or it'll be worse for you.'

Coulter suppressed a sigh and moved out to the sidewalk with the intention of entering the office, but, as he went forward, a voice hailed him from behind, and he paused and looked around to see Bill Swain emerging from an alley, followed closely by two townsmen carrying shotguns. Coulter moved back out of earshot of the office and Swain came up to him.

'The town council has agreed to suspend Coombe from his office,' the storekeeper said, 'and we're going to take over the law until the situation can be straightened out. I'm gonna put Coombe in a cell and hold him until enquiries have been made to discover the extent of his illegal actions. We'll take control of the jail and play it as it comes after that.'

'I'll give you a hand,' Coulter said instantly. 'Coombe and Doyle have got Julie in the office. I was about to go in after them.'

'Let me handle it,' Swain insisted. 'It's got to be done legally. There's been too much lawlessness around here already.'

'I'm only interested in Doyle,' Coulter said, 'and I don't think he'll give up without a fight. I'll cover him while you handle the sheriff.'

Swain nodded grimly as he drew a six-gun from his waistband and cocked it, saying: 'Let's go get them.'

'Just a minute.' Coulter glanced around the street. 'Mebbe you should tackle JH first. Coombe can wait, but JH hardcases are planning on taking Jethro Henderson out to his ranch, and when he's clear of town there'll be big trouble around here. Jessop is gonna start a clean-up of his own.'

Swain shook his head. 'We saw the buckboard at the rear of the hotel, and I decided it would be safer for the town to let Henderson go for the moment. We can consider what to do about him after we've secured the town and put an honest sheriff in Coombe's place.'

'OK.' Coulter checked the loads in his pistol. 'Let's get moving.'

Swain led the way to the law office, but when he tried the door he found it was locked. Coulter peered in through the broken window, lifted his gun over the still, and covered Doyle and Coombe. Swain knocked at the door and Doyle swung round, reaching for his pistol as he did so.

'Drop it, Doyle,' Coulter ordered, his voice rasping through the silence.

Doyle halted his draw, his fingers clenched around his gun butt. His fleshy face changed expression when he saw Coulter at the window, and a sickly grin appeared on his taut lips. For the space of a couple of heart beats he stared at Coulter, poised for action, and Coulter could almost read Doyle's thoughts in that eternal moment. Then

Doyle realized that as far as he was concerned the game was over, and completed his draw.

Coulter waited until Doyle's gun was clear of leather before triggering his Colt. The crash of the shot was ear-splitting. Gun smoke plumed through the window. Doyle jerked under the impact of the speeding chunk of lead that smacked into the centre of his chest. He swayed backwards, teetered on his heels, and then collapsed to the floor with his pistol spilling from his hand. Coulter shifted his aim to the lumbering sheriff, who overturned his chair in his hurry to rise.

Coombe's right hand reached swiftly for his gun, but he stayed the movement and let his hand fall to his side. Gun echoes were fading quickly. Coombe's eyes glittered.

'Hey, you're Wayne Coulter,' he said in a booming tone. 'Doyle was just talking about you. Maybe we can do some business together.'

'Sure.' Coulter smiled. 'Just lift your

gun off your hip and put it on the desk, then come and open the door. We can talk business.'

Swain had the sense to remain silent. Coulter watched Coombe lift his gun from its holster and toss it on his desk. The sheriff came around the desk and stepped over the prostrate Doyle, and Julie got up from her chair and ran to the desk to pick up the sheriffs discarded gun.

'You better do it right, Coombe, or you're dead,' Julie warned, cocking the gun.

Coombe paused and glanced over his shoulder. He returned his gaze to Coulter, noted the steady black muzzle of Coulter's gun covering him, and continued to the door. Coulter moved in behind Swain as the door swung open, and Coombe backed away into the office when he saw Swain and his two companions.

'What's going on?' Coombe demanded.

'Are you so stupid you don't see that your game is over?' demanded Swain.

He led the way into the office, followed closely by his two men, and Coulter followed, closing the office door at his back. Swain stuck the muzzle of his pistol into Coombe's bulging stomach.

'It's your turn to see the inside of a cell,' he said angrily. 'Your crooked deal is at an end. We'll have real law in this county now.'

'Do you think you can get away with this?' Coombe blustered.

'You know where the cells are, so on your way,' Swain retorted.

Coulter went to Doyle and bent over the outlaw. Doyle was dead, his fleshy face contorted, his eyes wide and staring. Coulter was satisfied that Blackjack Dawson could rest easy now, and straightened as Julie came to his side. Coombe was entering the cell block, followed closely by Swain.

'I'm sorry, Jack,' Julie said, her expression contrite. 'I do so want to help, but all I seem to be doing is making more trouble for you. I'll get my horse and ride out of town again, and this time I'll stay away until the trouble is over.'

'Now you're talking,' Coulter said with a flicker of a grin. 'I'll see you to your horse.'

'No, you won't,' a voice said from outside the broken window. 'Drop your gun, Wayne, and put your hands up.'

Coulter glanced quickly over his shoulder to see the grim face of Al Billing peering into the office, the muzzle of his pistol gaping at Coulter's chest.

'So you've done for Doyle,' Billing observed. 'I guess it's my turn next, if I give you the chance. I reckon I got to send you to Boot Hill, Wayne. I won't feel safe while you're still breathing.'

'I should have killed you earlier, Al,' Coulter replied.

'Yeah. Well, you've missed your chance. Now drop that gun and get your hands up. Where's the sheriff? He'll be pleased to see you under arrest.'

Coulter was between Julie and the window. The girl was holding Coombe's pistol in her hand, which was down at her side. Coulter released his hold on his pistol and it thudded on the floor and, at that instant, Julie cocked her pistol and threw up her arm to aim at Billing. The gun exploded, almost deafening Coulter, and orange muzzle flame spurted.

The bullet struck the window frame beside Billing's head and he ducked quickly. Coulter dropped to one knee, his right hand scrabbling desperately on the floor for his gun. Billing came up into view again, like a cork in a creek. Julie fired again. Coulter grasped his gun, swung it up to get into action, and discovered that he was staring into the muzzle of Billing's deadly gun . . .

10

Julie fired again, filling the office with gun noise. Smoke flared and echoes hammered. The bullet smacked into Billing's right shoulder and, as blood spurted, the outlaw twisted away, his gun falling from his hand. Coulter ran to the door and jerked it open to find Billing down on the sidewalk on one knee, clasping his shoulder. Coulter covered the outlaw.

'On your feet, Al,' he rasped, waggling his gun. 'You've had your last chance to pull out.'

Billing staggered to his feet. Blood was seeping from his wound. His face was ghastly pale in the light issuing from the office window. He glanced at his gun, lying out of reach on the sidewalk, shook his head, and entered the office. Coulter paused on the sidewalk to look around the street.

There was some movement in front of the hotel, where a couple of figures showed in the light issuing from the building, but they faded into the shadows even as Coulter spotted them. He stepped into the office to find Julie covering Billing with her gun.

Swain appeared in the doorway of the cell block. He grinned at the sight of Billing.

'I was wondering where you'd got to,' he remarked. 'Come this way. I've got a cell ear-marked for you.'

Billing disappeared into the cells. Coulter gazed at Julie, who looked completely exhausted. Her face was ashen, her lips taut, her eyes narrowed and filled with a harsh glitter. She met his gaze, and then raised her eyebrows in a silent question.

'I'm still wondering what to do with you for the best,' he said softly. 'I need to keep an eye on that wagon they're gonna take Henderson out of town in. Once it's clear of town I'll close in on it and kill Henderson, but I heard that

Jessop is gonna rake through the town to kill everyone against JH. So I've got to put you somewhere safe.'

'This time I'll find some dark corner and lie low until it's over,' she responded. 'I've had enough. I've come to the end of my rope. I can't go on like this.'

'That's more like it. I've been trying to get you away ever since we hit town.' Coulter grinned as he reloaded his gun.

Swain emerged from the cells. 'I'm gonna hang on in here until morning,' he said. 'With the crooked law department behind bars we've got a chance of beating Henderson.' He eyed the law badge pinned to Coulter's shirt. 'I don't know where you got that from, but if you raise your right hand I'll swear you in as a deputy. I have the power to do that, and I know you're the only man around here who is fighting Jethro Henderson.'

Coulter was shocked. He glanced at Julie, who nodded imperceptibly. He hesitated, and then raised his right hand. Swain swore him in.

'I guess your orders will be to carry on as you've been doing,' Swain said.

'Sure thing. I'll keep an eye on the activity around the hotel,' Coulter replied, 'and I'll kill Henderson if he sticks his nose outside the place.'

'It won't be over until Jethro is down in the dust,' Swain agreed, 'but you're only one man, so take it easy. You can't go against the whole JH outfit and expect to survive.'

'I haven't done too badly so far,' Coulter replied. 'I'll get on with it when Julie is in a safe place.'

A noise at the broken window caught Coulter's ears and he spun around to see two faces peering into the office. Lamplight glinted on blue steel as the newcomers thrust gun muzzles above the window sill. Coulter hurled himself sideways; his fast moving weight colliding with Julie and sending her crashing to the floor. Gun-flame spurted into the office and the thunder of rapid shots blasted the silence. Coulter drew his pistol as he hit the floor, and canted the muzzle to aim at the men outside.

Slugs thudded into the floor beside Coulter as he triggered his Colt. His eyes were narrowed, his teeth showing in a mirthless grin as he worked the mechanism of his gun. Splinters flew up from the window frame as his bullets struck at the attackers. One man fell away immediately with blood spraying from his face. The second man kept shooting, intent on killing, and his slugs crackled around Coulter but without scoring a hit.

Swain was caught flat-footed when the shooting started, and collected a slug in his chest. He dropped his gun, fell to his knees, and then sprawled forward on to his face. Coulter felt a red-hot flash of pain in the lobe of his left ear. The gunman at the window was angling his gun downwards and Coulter could see the black hole of the muzzle gaping at him. He triggered his gun and sent two slugs at the man, whose hammer clicked on a spent cartridge.

Coulter's bullets struck home and the man fell away.

The shooting ceased and gun echoes faded quickly. Coulter pushed himself to his feet, concerned about Julie, who was lying motionless at his side. He bent over her to find she was unconscious, and realized that she had struck her head on the side of the desk as she fell. He straightened and, as he reloaded his gun, he saw Swain lying on his back near the door to the cell block and crossed to him. Swain was dead.

The two men who had accompanied Swain were crouching behind the desk, and they got slowly to their feet when Coulter looked over at them.

'There's no future in this job,' said one of them. 'I'm getting out of here.'

'You've got a job to do,' Coulter said sharply.

'Not now Swain's dead.' The man gave a bitter laugh. 'It was Swain's idea to get involved. None of the other members of the town council wanted anything to do with it, and we're the only ones who decided to come along, but I reckon we should pull out.'

'I'll stick,' said the other man. 'I'm not running.'

'What's your name?' Coulter asked.

'Dave Turner. I'll take care of this place for you.'

'You're a fool, Dave.' The other man walked to the door and departed.

Julie groaned and began to stir. Coulter went to her side. He helped her into a sitting position as her eyes flickered open.

'It's all right,' he assured her gently. 'We're still winning all the tricks. But Swain is dead and one of his men has pulled out.'

He helped her into a seat and she put a hand to her head.

'You play rough,' she observed.

'Henderson's outfit is playing by the same rules,' he countered. 'When you're safely out of it I'll get back to taking on the gunnies.'

'I'll ride out of town,' she said. 'You won't have any more trouble from me.'

Coulter took her arm and helped her to arise. She staggered as she took the first steps towards the door, and then straightened and moved determinedly. He opened the door but went out first to the sidewalk to check that the way was clear. There were no signs of anyone on the street. He looked at Dave Turner, who had followed them to the door.

'I'll be back later,' he said, and Turner nodded, closed the door and locked it.

Coulter led the way to where Julie's horse was tied to a hitch rail.

'I'll head out in the opposite direction to Henderson's ranch,' she said tightening the saddle girth. 'I don't want to run into any of the JH bunch. I'll lie up outside of town, and come back tomorrow morning.'

'And don't let the sound of any shooting disturb you, huh?' Coulter suggested.

She mounted and shook her reins.

Coulter lifted a hand. He watched

her out of sight and, when the sound of departing hoofs had faded, he returned his attention to the job in hand. Entering an alley, he went along it to the back lots and made his way to the rear of the hotel.

A buckboard was standing outside the building, its team restless. There was no sign of anyone around, and Coulter halted in the shadows and forced himself to wait. The back door of the hotel was open, but there was no activity, and he drew his pistol and held it ready. The silence was overpowering. He leaned against a wall and tried to relax, aware of a nagging sensation in his chest. He wanted the fight to be over, wanted to be able to ride out of this town, pick up Julie, and pull out for good.

A man suddenly appeared in the back doorway of the hotel. He paused and peered around into the shadows, then went to the buckboard and climbed into the driving seat. As the horses were whipped into motion,

Coulter ran forward and jumped into the back of the wagon. He went forward to where the man was sitting and made his presence known by jabbing his gun between the man's shoulder blades.

'Keep going,' Coulter said harshly. 'What are you up to? Where's Jethro Henderson? Aren't you taking him back to the ranch in this wagon?'

'Jethro is a hard man, and he's decided that he ain't gonna run from no one. He's waiting for sun up, and then he'll come out on the street to face his enemies.'

'He'll be dead come sun up,' Coulter replied with a grin, 'and that goes for every man who rides for him.'

He struck the man with his gun barrel, and repeated the blow to render him fully unconscious. The team halted when the man dropped the reins, and Coulter vaulted over the side of the buckboard and ran to the nearest alley.

The street was still deserted when he paused in the alley mouth and looked around. He did not think he could get into the hotel and finish off Henderson while the man was surrounded by gunnies, but did not want to wait for the rancher to emerge in his own time. Thinking about it, Coulter returned to the back lots and went to the rear of Swain's store.

The store was locked. Coulter tried the back window, discovered that the catch was loose, and used his gun barrel to wrench the catch off the frame. He opened the window, climbed into the building, and went forward into the store, his nostrils filled with the many scents and smells of the merchandise. He struck a match, found a lantern and lit it, and held it high to look around. The reek of kerosene led him into a small room off to one side, where he saw a tank in a corner.

There were several cans beside the tank, and Coulter filled one with kerosene and departed with it. He went to the rear of the hotel and tried the back door, which opened to his touch. A lamp was alight nearby in the deserted passage that led to the front of the building. He moved stealthily, throwing kerosene around the passage and up the walls until the can was empty. Backing off, he picked up the lamp and hurled it along the passage into the centre of the spilled kerosene.

The kerosene ignited instantly. Flames roared greedily to encompass the deadly fluid. Coulter was forced to step outside the back door as the fire quickly took hold, and he watched for some moments, faintly surprised by the speed at which the flames spread. The woodwork was tinder-dry, and soon the whole passage was burning. Smoke billowed, and the heat drove Coulter away.

Coulter departed along the alley at the side of the hotel, reached the sidewalk, and moved in towards the big front door of the building. He walked through the entrance and saw two gunnies standing in the lobby. They covered him with their drawn pistols.

'Fire!' Coulter shouted the dreaded word at them. 'There's a blaze at the back of the hotel. Get everyone out.'

The men stared at him in shock, and then one of them turned and ran past the reception desk and through a doorway that led to the rear of the building.

'So you're a deputy,' said the remaining man. 'Where in hell is the sheriff? How come he ain't done nothing about that killer who's been shooting up our outfit?'

'I've been around town ever since sundown and ain't seen hide or hair of the polecat,' Coulter replied, 'but don't worry. We'll get him.'

The gunnie who had gone to check on the fire came back at a run, his face betraying shock.

'Someone splashed kerosene around the back,' he gasped. 'You can smell it. The whole rear of the hotel is alight, and it looks like nothing will stop it.'

'That damn killer again,' the other mused. 'He wants us to bring the boss out into the open so he can get a shot at him.'

'And you better move Henderson now or he won't get out,' Coulter said. 'That fire is spreading fast. I'll be watching the street for trouble. Get everybody out of the hotel, but fast.'

Coulter departed and crossed the street to an alley mouth opposite. He checked the gun in his holster, and also the second pistol stuck in his waistband. He could hear the two gunnies raising an alarm about the fire as he moved away, and soon the front doorway was crowded with fleeing figures. Coulter tensed, wanting to get his sights on just one man. He narrowed his eyes to pierce the gloom, and drew and cocked his pistol. The shooting was about to begin in earnest.

Several figures were appearing upon the balcony in front of Jethro Henderson's room. Coulter was tempted to open fire indiscriminately but restrained himself. He needed definite identification of the man he sought. Three men emerged from Henderson's room and stood on the balcony, watching the street. Lamplight flickered on their drawn weapons.

Certain that they were JH gunnies, Coulter opened fire on them. Gun smoke flew back into his face. One man fell instantly, and Coulter stepped back into the cover of the alley before the other two could return fire. He watched the front entrance, certain that Henderson would be brought out soon. Guns opened up at him from the balcony. He returned fire, and another man fell under his questing lead.

The doorway to the hotel cleared quickly, and two men began shooting from inside the lobby. Coulter shot down the third man on the balcony, and then directed his fire into the lobby. Bullets droned and snarled around the alley mouth. He fired at a gun flash, and one of the guns stopped shooting at him.

Silence followed in a lull that was filled with menace. Coulter could hear the crackling of the fire as it spread, and there was a red glow showing in the sky behind the building. Where was Jethro

Henderson? If they didn't bring him out soon they wouldn't get him out at all.

Two men appeared in the doorway of the hotel. One was wearing twin guns and his right arm was in a sling. It was Thad Henderson. Coulter lifted his pistol. The second man was Jessop. They came out to the edge of the sidewalk. Thad Henderson was carrying a shotgun with the butt tucked into his left armpit, the muzzle pointing at the ground. His head moved jerkily as he searched his surroundings.

'Over here,' Coulter yelled, half covered by a corner of the alley where he was standing. He thrust his gun hand forward as both men reacted fast to the sound of his voice.

Thad Henderson triggered his shot-gun, firing both barrels in a raucous explosion that sent more than 400 pellets in a deadly cone into the alley. But Coulter had stepped back into cover in the split second before the shooting started and the whirling loads of buckshot merely splintered the corner. He eased forward again, and two bullets from Jessop's gun crackled past his head. He triggered his Colt in furious reply, aiming each shot.

Thad Henderson was reloading the shotgun, and making a hard job of it. Coulter's first slug tore through Henderson's right shoulder. The shotgun pitched to the ground and Henderson awkwardly lifted his pistol from his left-hand holster. Coulter fired at Jessop, driving a slug into the centre of the man's chest. Jessop folded neatly at the waist and knees and dropped to the sidewalk on his knees. The pistol slipped from his suddenly nerveless hand, and then he fell forward on to his face in the dust of the street.

Thad Henderson sent two shots into the alley. Coulter felt a flash of red hot pain across his right forearm and almost dropped his pistol. He steadied himself and fired again. Henderson spun away and fell on the sidewalk. His heels drummed on the sunwarped boards before he became inert.

Coulter paused with gun uplifted, and gun smoke swirled around him. His throat was dry and his pulse was racing. He covered the street, waiting for the next move, and impatience began to stir inside him.

Smoke rose above the hotel as the fire spread rapidly. The echoes of the shooting dwindled away and, in the ensuing silence, Coulter could hear the crackling flames as they devoured the tinder-dry building. Sparks were flying from the conflagration, and despite the fact that the hotel was isolated by an alley on each side of it there was a big danger of the inferno spreading. There was no movement in the hotel now, and he began to wonder if Jethro Henderson was still in the building.

He remained in cover, reloaded his pistol, and watched for movement. He could see smoke issuing from the front windows of the hotel. The building was beyond saving, and Coulter realized that Jethro Henderson could not still be inside. The rancher had eluded a showdown . . .

Movement along the street attracted Coulter's attention, and he watched as a dozen townsmen advanced on the hotel and began to fight the fire. A manual pump was brought into action, and Coulter shook his head as he watched. The hotel was certainly doomed, and the fire fighters would be hard put to save the rest of the town.

He left his position and walked through the shadows towards the law office, wondering how he had missed Jethro Henderson's escape. It came to him that the rancher must have been moved out before he arrived to watch the hotel. Perhaps the buckboard out back had been a ruse to occupy his attention while the escape went ahead through the street entrance, or even by way of an alley window. But it mattered little because the time would come when he cornered Jethro Henderson and cut him down.

Coulter began to descend from the

high plateau of action and nerve that had been demanded by the fight, and became aware that he was exhausted, mentally and physically. He had not eaten at any time during the day, and he was thirsty. He paused and looked around, sensing that he had been robbed of total victory. He wanted to be able to tell Julie that Jethro Henderson was dead, but the rancher had been spirited away, and nothing was settled.

He reached the alley beside the law office and paused, still not convinced that Henderson had escaped. He leaned against the wall of the office, unutterably tired. He made an effort to move and, as he straightened, the door of the law office was opened and a dark figure emerged and came along the sidewalk. Coulter frowned as he palmed his Colt, for Dave Turner had been left alone in the office to guard the prisoners. He stuck the muzzle of his pistol into the man's side as he passed the alley.

'Hold it,' he rasped, lifting a six-gun from the man's holster. 'Who are you and what's your business?'

'Coulter?' Al Billing replied. 'Hell, it's just my luck to walk into you. Where did you spring from?'

'What are you doing out of your cell?'

'You made a bad choice when you left Turner in the office. He's one of Coombe's pards. He unlocked the cells and turned the office over to the sheriff the minute you left. Two of the JH outfit brought Jethro Henderson into the jail just before all that shooting started, and now the fight is over I've been sent out to find what happened at the hotel.'

Coulter's tiredness vanished at the news of Henderson. He grasped Billing's arm and drew the man away from the office.

'Don't hit me again, Wayne,' Billing said. 'I give up. I've had my fill of this burg. I'm toting a couple of bullet wounds already, and I want out of it. Let me go and I promise to ride to other parts with no more trouble.'

'No dice, Al. You're going back into

that office ahead of me to distract them, and you better hit the floor mighty quick when the lead starts flying.'

'Aw, hell, you don't need me,' Billing protested. 'I'd only get in your way. Let me ride out. You don't want me under your feet.'

'How many in the jail?' Coulter's mind was already leaping ahead to action.

'Coombe, Jethro Henderson, and Turner. Look, if I walk back into that office I'll be the first to collect a slug. Don't do this to me, Wayne.'

'Stop your belly-aching. You had plenty chances to get clear but you wouldn't go. So let's get to it.'

'OK. Gimme a gun and I'll help you clean 'em out. I'll do it for five hundred bucks.'

'No gun,' Coulter insisted. 'You go in first to cover me, and then you hit the floor so I can get the drop on them. Now move. I've got to get this done.'

Billing shrugged and turned back to the office. Coulter followed closely. Billing paused with his hand on the door handle and glanced back at Coulter, who jabbed him in the back with his pistol.

'No tricks, Al,' he warned.

Billing thrust open the law office door and entered the office. Coulter moved in behind, keeping himself covered by the outlaw's bulky figure. He peered over Billing's broad shoulder and saw Sheriff Coombe seated at his desk. Dave Turner was seated on a chair beside the desk, and Jethro Henderson was half lying on the floor in a corner on a mattress taken from a cell. The JH rancher was holding a 12 gauge double-barrelled shotgun in his hands. He was pale, wild-looking, and had a bloodstained bandage around his chest and left shoulder.

'I told you to check out the street, Billing,' Coombe rasped in his booming voice as he looked up. 'What are you doing back here? You ain't had time to look around. Get out there again and see if you can find that pard of yours. We want him.'

'Who's behind you, Billing?' Dave Turner demanded, springing up and snatching at a pistol lying on the desk.

Billing dropped to the floor, leaving Coulter facing the opposition.

Coombe sprang up, overturning his chair in his haste, and his holstered gun seemed to flow into his hand. Coulter fired at Turner, whose weapon exploded a split second after Coulter's gun blasted, sounding almost as an echo. The office shook with the double gun blast. Coulter heard Turner's slug crackle by his head, and dropped to one knee as Turner twisted and fell backwards with blood showing on his shirt front. The sheriff brought his pistol into the aim, grimacing as he tried to get into the fight.

Coulter squeezed his trigger when his foresight covered the sheriff's belt buckle. His gun bucked and the bullet sped straight and true at the big figure of the crooked lawman. Coombe yelled in a high-pitched voice when the slug struck him, and struggled desperately to level his gun at Coulter, but firing a shot was too much for him. His legs gave way suddenly and he dropped to the floor on his knees, leaning his arms on the desk to remain in a kneeling position, but his Colt was too heavy for his failing strength and he dropped it, then fell sideways and disappeared from view behind the desk.

Coulter turned his gun towards Henderson, who was having trouble using his wounded shoulder. The shotgun in the rancher's hands was lifting to cover Coulter, who judged that he would be too slow to stop the deadly weapon from covering him. He thrust his pistol forward, his teeth clenched and muscles tensed for a burst of buckshot, and at that instant a rifle cracked behind him from outside the open window and a .44-.40 slug bored into Jethro Henderson's chest. The rancher jerked under the impact and lost his grip on the shotgun as he fell back dead.

Coulter's ears were protesting at the

noise of the shooting as he spun around to see Julie's tense face peering through the broken window. His tension fled and he lowered his smoking gun. Tiredness seemed to rush in on him from all sides.

'It looked pretty close between you and Henderson,' Julie said, 'and I couldn't take a chance with him holding a shotgun. It's a good thing I stuck around, huh?'

Coulter nodded. 'It's all done,' he said quietly, his ears throbbing, 'and I can't believe I'm still alive. I was sure I was riding the trail to Boot Hill.'

'If it's all over then I'm going home,' Julie told him. 'I've got a ranch to get back to. What are you going to do, Jack? I've been telling everyone that you work for me, but if you have other plans then that's OK.'

'No.' Coulter spoke sharply. 'I've got a hunch that I'd be better off sticking with you. You never know, I might get shot again some time in the future, and I sure wouldn't want anyone but you to nurse me.'

'Come on then.' Julie smiled. 'Our horses are waiting together. Let's go get them and ride.'

Al Billing was getting up from the floor. He dusted himself down and grinned at Coulter.

'What about me?' he demanded.

'Do what we are gonna do,' Coulter replied. 'Ride out, but fast, and in a different direction. I'm turning over a new leaf, Al, and you'd be wise to do the same.'

'Sure thing.' Billing opened the door and departed.

Coulter left the office and fell into step with Julie as they went for their horses, and she took his arm as they walked through the shadows. The smell of smoke was strong in the town but the breeze was busy blowing it away, and Coulter found his thoughts drifting hopefully to the future for the first time since he had been shot.

We do hope that you have enjoyed reading this large print book.

Did you know that all of our titles are available for purchase?

We publish a wide range of high quality large print books including:
Romances, Mysteries, Classics
General Fiction
Non Fiction and Westerns

Special interest titles available in large print are:
The Little Oxford Dictionary
Music Book, Song Book
Hymn Book, Service Book

Also available from us courtesy of Oxford University Press:
Young Readers' Dictionary
(large print edition)
Young Readers' Thesaurus
(large print edition)

For further information or a free brochure, please contact us at:
Ulverscroft Large Print Books Ltd.,
The Green, Bradgate Road, Anstey,
Leicester, LE7 7FU, England.
Tel: (00 44) **0116 236 4325**
Fax: (00 44) **0116 234 0205**

HAL GRANT'S WAR

Elliot James

When Hal Grant's father was bushwhacked in the street, it was the opening shot of a range war. Wealthy ranchers were determined to rid Lundon County of its sharecroppers and sodbusters eking out an existence in the marginal lands. Hal should have sided with his fellow ranchers, but he did not believe in mob law. He was caught in the middle — and no one was allowed to sit on the fence in a conflagration that was consuming a county . . .

THEY CALLED HIM LIGHTNING

Mark Falcon

A blow to the head had caused him memory loss and temporary blindness. Was he Mike Clancey, the name inscribed on the pocket watch he carried? And the beautiful woman's picture on the inside of the watch — was she his wife? He needed answers. Known as Lightning for his gun skills, riding Thunder, a black gelding, with fair play and talent he would bring a tyrant to justice — but it was a dangerous trail he must follow.

HOMESTEADERS' WAR

Tom Parry

When Wilbur Daniels and his fellow homesteaders are faced with tax demands from the Crossville council, they are up in arms. However, they find support from the ex-sheriff, Luke Tilling, a drunkard who is suffering from a personal tragedy. As bullets begin to fly, a powerful landowner seizes his chance of getting rid of the homesteaders. Not even the beautiful Cordelia can prevent Luke from taking his life in his hands. Will he survive, or will tragedy strike again?

RETURN TO BLACK ROCK

Scott Connor

Despite being innocent, Glenn Price served fifteen years for his father's murder. However, immediately upon his release, he is captured by bounty hunter Randall Nash. Glenn is dragged back to Black Rock, where the townsfolk nearly lynched him before, and soon faces the mob again when the corrupt sheriff charges him with another unjustified allegation of murder. Can Glenn clear his name and find the real killer before the townsfolk invite him to a necktie party?

COLT HEAT

Matt James

Wiley, a loner, was the cool, cold king of the .45s. He had no friends and few women, and was the nemesis of the danger trails until he drifted into Missoula, a bloody frontier town at war with itself. His crashing .45s announced who and what he was. Only Vestal Lee saw the real man behind the killing guns. But before she could tame him, the shooting war engulfed Missoula, with Wiley in the blazing front line of battle.

NIGHTMARE PASS

Lance Howard

Marshal Galen Trimble is a hero: single-handedly he brought down the Crigger Gang, ending the so-called 'scarecrow murders'. But years later when he's targeted by an unknown killer, resurrecting the same *modus operandi*, people speculate that a lost Crigger brother is exacting his revenge. Now, as Trimble's old riding buddy Jim Hannigan and his lovely partner are ʾrought into the investigation, their ʾssion to find the killer will unlock ʾoor to the past that alters their ʾuture.